SECOND HAND
A TUCKER SPRINGS NOVEL

HEIDI **CULLINAN**
MARIE **SEXTON**

Riptide Publishing
PO Box 6652
Hillsborough, NJ 08844
www.riptidepublishing.com

Second Hand (Tucker Springs, #2)

Cover Art by L.C. Chase, lcchase.com/design.htm
Editor: Sarah Frantz
Layout: L.C. Chase, lcchase.com/design.htm

ISBN: 978-1-937551-52-0
First edition
September, 2012

Also available in ebook:
ISBN: 978-1-937551-57-5

SECOND HAND
A TUCKER SPRINGS NOVEL

HEIDI CULLINAN
MARIE SEXTON

RIPTIDE
PUBLISHING

For Marpy, because she deserves it.

TABLE OF CONTENTS

CHAPTER 1

Going into the pawnshop was a mistake. I knew it the same way I'd known two months before that Stacey was going to leave me, some nagging sense of unease deep in the pit of my stomach. On the day she'd left, I'd stopped on my way home and bought dinner because a little voice in the front of my brain chattering away like a chipmunk refused to believe that sense of impending doom. It insisted that chow mein and sweet and sour pork would make Stacey smile and everything would be all right.

Of course, the chipmunk had been stilled to silence by the empty house and the note on the bedroom door.

The chipmunk, however, never learned. Today my inner rodent had prattled on, reminding me Stacey's birthday was in two days. I couldn't not get her a present, it reasoned, not after all the time we'd had together. Worse, how could I pass up a chance to win her back?

Of course, I was looking to buy said present at a pawnshop. This was a new level of desperation, even for the chipmunk.

I opened the door of the pawnshop but stopped dead when I got a good look inside. The neon lights outside flashing "BUY - SELL - PAWN" should have tipped me off as to what kind of atmosphere I'd find, but I'd never actually been in a pawnshop before, and it was far worse than I'd anticipated. It was dirty and cluttered and sad. Discarded items—mostly TVs, stereos, and Blu-ray players—lay dead on the shelves. An entire wall held musical instruments, silent in the absence of their owners. The smell of cigarette smoke and something else lingered in the air, something I couldn't identify. Something that reeked of failure. I was overwhelmed by the same sense of helplessness I felt at the animal shelter, all the animals behind bars, wondering why nobody loved them anymore.

I almost turned and walked back out, but the man sitting behind the counter was watching me, his booted feet on the glass display with a half-smoked cigarette drooping between his lips.

"Can I help you?" he asked, and I marveled at the way the cigarette stayed stuck in the side of his mouth.

I shoved my hands into my pants pockets. "I'm looking for jewelry."

He took the butt out of his mouth and smiled at me as he stood. "You've come to the right place, my friend."

I doubted that, but I chose not to contradict him. The "right place" would have been the jewelry store down the street, its windows full of gold and diamonds, but I sure as hell couldn't afford that. One of the downtown art galleries had beautiful glass pendants, but the chipmunk had protested. They were colorful, but twisted glass wouldn't win Stacey back.

The owner led me around the shop through a faint haze of cigarette smoke, past glass cases full of iPods and cameras, GPS navigators and laptops, to one along the back wall that held jewelry. The selection was crazily eclectic. Giant turquoise bracelets and dainty gold chains, wedding bands and strings of pearls.

"You looking for anything in particular?" he asked.

That was a good question. What should I buy? Not a ring. I'd already given her one of those. Never mind that it was currently sitting in a bowl on my bedside table. Not a bracelet. She didn't like them because they got in her way when she worked.

"A necklace?" I asked.

"Don't sound so sure of yourself." He stuck what was left of the cigarette into the side of his mouth, squinting against the ribbon of smoke that rose past his eyes as he unlocked the cabinet and began to pull out the displays of necklaces. The smoke curled around the coarse twists of his hair.

"Are you allowed to smoke in here?" I asked.

He glanced up at me, almost smiling. His black hair was shaved short on the sides and in the back, but the top was longer, spiked straight up in a way that hinted more at laziness than style. He was one of those casually cool guys, I realized, who were naturally put-together and suave, who found everybody else slightly amusing. And slightly stupid. "My store."

"Yeah, but aren't there city ordinances or something?"

He took the butt out of his mouth and leaned both hands on the edge of the glass counter to look at me. He was taller than me. Thin, though. Not bulky at all, but he still managed to make me feel small. "Pretty sure I'm the only honest pawnbroker in town. As long as I'm not fencing, cops don't exactly care about my personal vices."

"I see." I tried to hide my embarrassment by looking down at the necklaces.

"Is this for your mom or a girlfriend?"

"Girlfriend," I said, deciding he didn't need to know about the "ex" part of the equation.

"In that case, I'd say stay away from pearls and Black Hills gold." He shrugged and rubbed his hand over the hair at the nape of his neck. "They're sort of old school. Opals, too."

"She likes sapphires."

"Show me a woman who doesn't." He knocked the cherry off his cigarette onto the concrete floor, rubbed it out with his foot, and tossed the butt in the trash can before pointing to a necklace in the center. It had a stone so dark blue it was almost black. "This is the only sapphire I have right now, but if you want my opinion, it sort of screams 1995. Now this," he pointed to one near the end, "this one is new. Platinum's all the rage, you know."

"Platinum?" I touched the necklace. It looked like silver to me, but I wasn't exactly an expert on jewelry. The stone appeared to be a large rectangular diamond, surrounded by a bunch of smaller round ones. "It looks expensive."

"*Looks* being the operative word." He smiled and crossed his arms over his chest. "The platinum is real, but the diamonds aren't."

"They're fake?"

"Cubic zirconium. Just as pretty, but way more affordable than the real thing."

I wasn't sure about giving Stacey imitation stones, but it was definitely the nicest necklace he had. Even used, it was more than I could really afford, but that chipmunk in my brain was enamored with it, positive it was the only thing Stacey would want.

"I can pay you half in cash and half on my card. Is that okay?"

"No personal checks, but cash and credit both work."

"Do you have some kind of nice box or something it can go in?"

He laughed, revealing perfect teeth that seemed extra white against his bronze skin. "No, I'm gonna give it to you in a Ziploc baggie." I wasn't really sure what to say to that, but he laughed again. "I'm kidding. Yeah, I got a box around here somewhere. You think I'm running some kind of second-rate establishment?"

The way he said it, it wasn't a challenge. He seemed to be mocking himself more than anything, admitting that of course this was a second-rate store. That was, after all, the entire idea of a pawnshop. Second owner. Second hand.

I hoped very much that in my case, it would mean a second chance.

CHAPTER 2

El watched the necklace-buyer leave, trying not to laugh at the absurdity of it all. The whole thing had "long-term disaster" stamped all over it. Sometimes his customers were desperate. Sometimes stupid. This one? Mostly he'd seemed perpetually confused.

When his cell phone rang, El was still smiling, thinking about Clueless Joe as he answered. "Tucker Pawn."

"Aren't we all bright and cheery this evening?" Denver Rogers's voice was rough, full of drawl that didn't quite come from the South. "If my ears don't deceive me, you might actually be smiling. You take someone home and get snuggly last night?"

"I don't snuggle."

"Well, something's got you sounding like Suzie Sunshine."

El smiled at the image of the necklace-buyer as Suzie Sunshine. Oddly, he kind of was. "Just a customer."

"Oh?" There was a world of innuendo in that single syllable.

"*Just* a customer." Brownish-red hair, pale skin, little freckles across his nose. El couldn't help but imagine the soft, white skin in the places that didn't see the sun. "He was damn cute, though."

Denver whistled through his teeth. "Well, goddamn. Somebody call the *Tucker Gazette*. Emanuel Mariano Rozal is showing signs of humanity. Next thing you know, he might settle down and start collecting cats."

"Whatever."

"So we on tonight, or what?"

"Looks like *or what*."

Denver's huff belied his irritation, and El could picture him scowling. The two of them had a weekly "date" at the Tucker Laund-O-Rama, which wasn't nearly as kinky as it sounded. It had nothing in the world to do with sex, and everything to do with having somebody over the age of twenty-two to talk to while their socks ran the spin cycle.

"What is it this time?" Denver asked.

"I told Rosa I'd watch the kids."

"Come on, man. Your entire fucking family, and she picks you?"

"Miguel's on call for the fire department, and his wife can barely deal with their own kids. Rosa's fighting with Lorenzo's wife—"

"About what?"

"I'm doing my best not to know." If there was one thing El had learned, it was not to get involved in family drama. Especially when it came to the women. *Especially* when it came to his little sister Rosa, who made the stereotype of the fiery Latina woman look like Tinkerbell. "She's been leaving them with her neighbor, but she got busted for possession—"

"Nice."

"That leaves Abuela, and she's too old to have to deal with those little shits on her own."

"What about your mom?"

Leave it to Denver to notice the person El had left off his list. "Look man, it's me. I said I'd do it."

Denver sighed. "Someday, you're going to wake up and wish you'd gotten out from behind that counter a bit more."

"And you're going to wish you hadn't bulked up on 'roids." El was pretty sure Denver didn't actually use steroids, but when a man was built like a fucking barn, he could take a bit of ribbing.

"Why can't you bring the kids along?"

"You serious?"

"Why not? They might liven things up a bit."

El thought about Rosa's three kids running around the laundromat. They'd scare away any little frat boys in a heartbeat, no doubt about it. "You're on. Eight o'clock?"

"Sounds good."

"Hey, Denver?"

"Yeah?"

"I don't snuggle."

He laughed. "Fine. But I take back that 'signs of humanity' remark. You're as much of an asshole as ever."

El had thought he was watching the kids because Rosa had to work, but when he showed up at her house at 6:30, he found her wearing tight black jeans and high-heeled boots and displaying a whole lot of cleavage. Not exactly the sort of thing she'd wear to wait tables, not even at Giuseppe's.

"Christ, Rosa. Put on a sweater or something."

She hooked her hands under her breasts and lifted them a bit. "Fuck off, bro."

"You didn't tell me it was a date."

"You didn't ask."

True enough. The fact was, the less El thought about what his sister got up to, the better. He was sure the feeling was mutual. "Who is he this time?"

She turned away to study her hair in the mirror. "Somebody I met."

"No shit, Captain Obvious. Where at?"

"Out."

He sighed and sat down on her couch. "You got three kids by three different dads, and not one of those sperm donors is worth a damn. When you gonna learn?"

"Just because you don't date doesn't mean I can't." She pinched her cheeks and reached for a tube of lipstick. "I ain't cut out to be a nun."

Which meant El was a monk. Which wasn't entirely off the mark, which annoyed the hell out of him. "Do you ever stop to think about where you're going and what you're doing? Do you ever think of the future? Your kids' future, maybe with a stable male role model in the picture?"

She bared her teeth at him in the mirror. "Oh, but sweetheart, if they need a male stick-in-the-mud, they can look to Uncle Emanuel." She yelled down the hallway, "Let's go, kids. I got places to be."

"And men to do," El said under his breath.

The only acknowledgement El received was a middle finger flipped his way.

"What do you care that she's on a date?" Denver asked El two hours later as they loaded clothes into side-by-side washing machines.

El glanced around to make sure Rosa's kids weren't listening. They weren't. They were running around the laundromat, playing hide-and-seek among the tables and chairs. The only other person around was a young woman wearing skin-tight sweatpants with Greek letters across her ass. She had on headphones and was handily ignoring the world.

"It's not that it's a date," El told Denver. "It's that she's being an idiot."

Denver slammed the door to his washer and glanced sideways at El as he thumbed quarters into the machine. "You're the most judgmental person I know."

"It's not my fault people are stupid."

"Am I included in that assessment, Mr. Genius?"

El sighed and slammed his own washer shut. "Look. When she's hurt and crying because another loser has left, she comes clean and tells me what she really wants. She says she wants a nice guy who'll settle down with her. Take care of her and take care of the kids. Come to family dinners and help Abuela when she needs it. Somebody who'll be part of the family."

"Makes sense." Denver shrugged and glanced down at the floor, his voice gruff as he added, "Nothing wrong with wanting that."

"I'm not saying it's wrong. But look at it this way: you work at Lights Out. Biggest, gayest club in town, right?"

"Yeah."

"And you're standing here saying you wouldn't mind finding somebody to settle down with, right?"

Denver's jaw tensed and he took a step back. "I never said—"

"My point is, you have a couple hundred gay boys to pick from every night. But you don't."

Denver relaxed a bit, probably because he knew El wasn't about to hound him on the settling down thing. "Club's nothing but college boys looking to get laid."

"Exactly." El turned away to put his money into the slots. "Men in the straight clubs are no different. She meets these guys at the bar, takes them home within a week, then wonders why they turn out to be losers."

"Where's she supposed to meet them?"

"I don't know. PTA meetings. Church. The grocery store." El waved his hands to indicate the walls around them. "The fucking laundromat."

Denver snorted. "I take it she don't go to those places?"

"She does, actually, and guys ask her out, but you know what she says? She says they're old or they're fat. Or maybe they're going bald. So she keeps choosing these drunken asshats at the bar, then wondering why they don't turn out to be Mr. Right."

"You think Mr. Right's hanging out at Tucker Laund-O-Rama?"

Of course, when he said it that way, it sounded pretty stupid. "Maybe. Yeah."

Denver raised his eyebrows. "Do me a favor, El. Let me know when he walks in the door."

CHAPTER 3

When I got home after work, I saw someone had stuck a bright pink flier into the rickety screen on my front door. I left it on the kitchen counter while I dialed Stacey's number.

No answer.

I stared at the flier as the phone rang. *Curb Appeal Contest*, it read. Although houses in similar neighborhoods in Tucker Springs were in high demand, my little corner, an older section between the edge of the Light District and the railroad tracks, was slowly falling into disrepair. The self-appointed homeowner's association was always trying to come up with ways to increase property value. Block parties. New playgrounds. It seemed this time it was a drive to improve the look of the lawns and houses in the neighborhood. I was about to toss it aside when the bottom line caught my eye. *$500 cash prize.*

I could use $500. No doubt about that.

I dialed Stacey's number again. Still no answer.

I put on some music and stuck a frozen dinner in the microwave, wondering how much it would take to win the contest.

Our secret judges will be patrolling the neighborhood, looking for yards that are well kept, colorful, and inviting.

That didn't sound too hard. And for a cash prize—

There was a dull *pop*, and the kitchen went dim and silent.

"Goddammit." I shoved away from the counter and glared at the faded wallpaper as if I could bore through to the wires beneath. "Should have known."

I'd long suspected the wiring in the house had never been up to code and that whatever work had been done on it hadn't exactly been on the level. The annoyances of living in a place where half of the wiring consisted of duct tape and extension cords were part of my daily life. No running the microwave and the window-unit air conditioner at the same time. No using the computer while watching TV. Every time Stacey had used her blow dryer in the tiny master bathroom, the bedroom lights flickered and my alarm clock blinked until I reset it.

With a weary sigh, I went into the garage and flipped the breaker. Back in the kitchen, I turned off the AC and restarted the microwave, then went back to the flier.

The contest would run for a month. They even had a website where weekly scores would be displayed. It was worth a shot, right?

I called Stacey again. This time, she picked up.

"Hello?"

She sounded annoyed. My heart sank. "Hey, Stacey. Happy birthday."

"Paul, you shouldn't be calling. I've told you that. If Larry finds out—"

"Well, I certainly wouldn't want to upset your new boyfriend," I said, unable to keep the bitterness out of my voice.

She sighed. "What do you want?"

This definitely wasn't going the way I had hoped. The microwave beeped, signaling that my dinner was ready. Why hadn't I waited until afterward to call?

I took a deep breath. "I wondered if you're free tomorrow night? I wanted to take you out to dinner for your birthday. We could—"

"No."

"It's only dinner."

"I really can't. Larry wouldn't like it."

"Come on, Stacey. After seven years together, I'm not even allowed to wish you happy birthday?"

"You just did. And I appreciate it. But dinner isn't a good idea."

I opened the microwave door, waving away the steam. "How about lunch, then?"

She sighed, and I knew she was about to say no.

"Coffee?"

"I don't know, Paul. I—"

Whatever she said after that, I didn't hear, because my smoke detector went off. It was loud and high-pitched, as all smoke detectors seemed to be, and I jumped.

"*Shit.* Hang on, I'll be right back."

"Paul? Are you okay?"

Too angry to answer, I put the phone down and went through the usual routine of making the noise stop. I couldn't reach the smoke detector on the ceiling, but I took off my shirt and waved it at the thing, jumping up and down, trying to scatter whatever hint of smoke it thought it smelled. The damn thing went off nearly every time I cooked, whether I managed to burn my food or not.

"Shut up," I yelled at it. I swung my shirt again, and it caught the edge of the lid and pulled it open. The incessant whine of the alarm stopped, although my ears were still ringing.

It hardly seemed fair that Stacey had picked the house and then left me to deal with it, although if I had my way, she'd be coming back.

"Fire alarm, huh?" she asked when I picked up the phone again. "Hasn't the landlord fixed that yet?"

"Of course not. Listen, Stacey, couldn't you at least meet me for a cup of coffee?"

"I don't know."

"Please?"

She sighed. She was relenting.

"Just coffee," I emphasized, taking the window she'd left open. "How about after work tomorrow?"

It took her a moment, but she finally said, "Fine. Coffee. I can be at Mocha Springs at five."

That would mean I'd have to skip out of work early, but I'd figure it out. "Great. I'll see you then."

She'd already hung up the phone.

I'd always wanted to be a veterinarian, but that wasn't how things had worked out. Instead, I was a glorified receptionist at a veterinary office. On the bright side, my boss, Nick Reynolds, was a great guy.

"Hey, Doc," I said to him. "Is it okay if I cut out a bit early today?" Normally on Thursdays, we closed the office at five, and I'd be there another half hour or so wrapping things up, but I didn't want to be late for my date with Stacey.

I wasn't sure if Nick had a date tonight too, but I assumed he did. Though we were nearly the same age—early thirties—Nick was successful, handsome, and built. I suspected women threw themselves at him.

"How early?" he asked.

"Maybe quarter to five or so?"

He shrugged. "Yeah, I think I can manage." He tossed the patient file he'd been reviewing on my desk and leaned back with his elbows on the counter behind him. The motion stretched his shirt across his chest in a way that would have made many a coed swoon. "You got a hot date?"

I looked down at the file so he wouldn't notice me checking him out. Nice chest. Tattoos up one arm. He was attractive and funny and nice, and that made him intimidating as hell.

Not that I was gay or anything. I just happened to notice he looked very nice.

"I'm meeting Stacey. It's her birthday."

He didn't say anything, and when I looked back up, he was shaking his head. "You're a glutton for punishment."

"I just think—"

"It's cool," he said, turning to pick up the next file on the stack. "I don't mind you leaving."

"Thanks, Nick."

He glanced over at me again. He raised his eyebrows and opened his mouth as if he were about to say something, but then the bell on the door rang and his next client came in.

"Hey, Seth," Nick said, reaching across the counter to shake the man's hand. He nodded at the pet carrier the man held. "How's Stanley?"

"Fatter than ever."

Nick laughed. "Somehow I'm not surprised." He motioned to the door that led to the exam room. "Go on back. I'll be with you in a minute."

Once he was gone, Nick turned to look at me. He had insanely blue eyes. Almost as blue as Stacey's. "Listen, kid, it's not my business, but if you want my advice on Stacey—"

"I don't."

Because I'd heard it before. I was better off without her. She was bad news. Move on.

He sighed. "Okay. Fair enough. I guess in that case, I wish you good luck."

"Thanks, Nick."

He shook his head as he turned to leave the room. "God knows you're going to need it."

The coffee shop Mocha Springs Eternal sat a couple of blocks over from Nick's office in the foot mall the Light District was known for. I passed the pawnshop and crossed to the cobblestone walkways that made up the center of downtown. It was a gorgeous evening, near eighty degrees but with a soft cool breeze that suited the outdoor atmosphere of the mall. A man strummed an acoustic guitar on a bench while teenagers skateboarded right past the "Dismount Zone" signs. Couples strolled hand in hand, some traditional boy-girl, but many same-sex couples as well. We hadn't realized until after we'd rented the house that we were smack in the middle of Tucker Springs's version of the Castro. Stacey had been embarrassed, as if we were intruding where we weren't wanted, but I liked it. The atmosphere in the Light District was bright and fun and friendly.

The ice cream parlor was packed. Kids sat out front, racing to finish their ice cream in the sun. Their sticky little hands clutched waffle cones. Ice cream dripped from their chins. Parents laughed at the foolishness of trying to wipe them clean. I smiled, thinking about them as I passed a series of art galleries and novelty shops, a martini bar, and a designer dress shop. Finally, I arrived at Mocha Springs Eternal.

I checked the bar by the front window, the tables along the brick wall, and the couches in back. Stacey hadn't yet arrived. I bought a cup of coffee for myself and a raspberry mocha cappuccino for her, and took one of the open tables near the front, where we could watch the people passing by. She liked to people-watch.

She came in, and I waved her over to my table. She'd cut her hair shorter than I'd ever seen it, and dyed it platinum instead of the dirty dishwater blonde it had been since I'd known her. A clunky shell necklace was visible under the collar of her blouse. "Hello," she said as she sat down with her back to the front window. "How've you been?"

"Good," I lied. "Happy birthday." I slid the foam-topped mug across the table. "I got you your usual."

She looked down at it and wrinkled her nose. "It's not my usual anymore. Too many calories. I drink chai now."

"Oh."

She sniffed and nervously touched the side of her eye, first one, then the other. She was wearing makeup—eyeliner, shadow, and thick mascara. When we'd been together, she'd only worn makeup like that for parties or evenings out. Never during the day.

I fought down the disappointment that welled up in my chest. "Seems like everything about you has changed."

She tapped her finger on the table.

I took a drink of my lukewarm coffee and tried a new tactic. "How's your work going?"

She relaxed marginally, leaning back in her chair. "I'm finishing up another sculpture. I've been showing my portfolio around, and there's a consignment gallery in Estes Park that may be interested."

"That's great," I said, although the words were like sand in my throat. We'd come to Tucker Springs specifically because it was artsy, and Stacey had thought she'd be able to sell the scrap metal monstrosities she called art. I knew I should tell her good luck, but any connections she was making in Estes were probably through Larry, the man who had replaced me. I'd moved here to make her happy, and she'd moved on without a backward glance.

"Are you still working for Dr. Reynolds?" she asked.

I nodded, unsure what to say. The box with the necklace was wedged into my front pants pocket. I could feel its bulk against my thigh. "I bought you something." I kept my eyes down so I didn't have to see the exasperation in her eyes. I took the box out and slid it across the table to her. "For your birthday."

"You shouldn't have done that."

She was right. After buying the necklace, I'd imagined giving it to her. I'd pictured her being surprised and appreciative, smiling and pleased, but the folly of that belief was now painfully clear. She had a new life. A new hairdo. A new lover. She didn't want diamonds, fake or real.

She didn't want me.

Nick was right. I was a fool. A glutton for punishment. I wished desperately I'd never bought the necklace at all. I was about to reach across and take the box back, but I was too slow. She picked it up and opened it.

"Jesus, Paul," she said in disgust. "What were you thinking?"

"I thought you'd like it."

"I can't accept this." She snapped the box shut and put it on the table between us. "Thank you for the thought, but really, you shouldn't have bought it." She pinched the bridge of her nose, shaking her head. "I shouldn't have come."

The words I'd planned to say died in my throat. *I'd hoped to have a chance to talk about things. Maybe if you came home, we could work things out.*

"Don't call anymore," she said as she stood up. "And don't buy me any more gifts."

Going home after my date with Stacey was like pouring lemon juice on an open wound.

I stood on the sidewalk in front of the house for a solid fifteen minutes, forcing myself to document every reminder of her I had, starting with the outside of our home. The house itself was her doing, a cute tri-color bungalow that looked like a gingerbread house with a modern twist. Her curtains decorated the windows, custom ones she'd ordered even though we hadn't bought the place. We'd signed a three-year lease, or rather, I'd signed it, which was why I'd be stuck here for another eighteen months, minimum.

The outdoor decor was Stacey's too, all of it failed sculptures or projects that'd never panned out. In addition to the faux barbed wire she'd called "anti-edging"—a failed entrepreneurial idea she'd dumped into the flowerbeds—two of her unsold sculptures stood in our front lawn. One was a seven-foot-tall flower, its stem made from a car bumper, its petals from garishly painted hubcaps, and its leaves from rearview mirrors. She'd called it *Detroit Daisy*. It was possibly her best work, which wasn't saying much.

The other was harder to describe. It was some kind of cross between a dinosaur and a chicken standing on one leg and wearing a cowboy boot. I'd forgotten its title. It was taller than me, and I thought it was horrific, but of course I'd never told her that. Both sculptures seemed to mock me as I made my way to the front door.

The house was empty, of course. Stacey swore she was allergic to all animals—cats, dogs, and birds, anything I'd named. I'd always thought it was psychosomatic, but I'd never said anything about that either.

The inside of the house was a little better, as Stacey's taste in furniture was pretty standard, though each piece she'd selected reminded me of her. As I stood there feeling sorry for myself and my failures, I remembered how much I'd let her call the shots in our relationship, and I decided it was time for that to stop, since she wasn't here anymore.

My first act of defiance was to park my butt in front of the TV and zone out until it was time for bed. It wasn't much, and I wasn't sure it was exactly defiance since Stacey probably wouldn't have told me I couldn't do it, but it still felt good. Maybe it was defiance because I didn't let myself spend the night obsessing over what I'd done wrong with her. As rebellions went, it was paltry, but I supposed we all had to start somewhere.

Nick was nice enough not to ask about my date with Stacey the next morning, although I did catch him watching me out of the corner of his eye. I kept my head down and chose not to fill him in on how right he'd been.

It was a shitty day at the office all around, not only because of my epic failure as a boyfriend the night before, but also because we had to put down two different animals that day. Both were old, and loved, one a cat who could no longer eat because of late-stage cancer, the other a dog whose arthritis had grown so bad he could barely stand. In both cases, it was probably for the best, but it still broke my heart. I was glad their owners both went back and held them as it was done. The ones who dropped the animals off and left always made me angry. Stacey had told me many times that I was too soft, and maybe it was true, because I hated to see any life having to end. Both times I ended up in the bathroom, washing the evidence of tears off my cheeks.

I couldn't quite face my empty house again after work. Instead, I grabbed the necklace and walked downtown to the heart of the Light District. It was a bit cooler than it had been the day before, but still plenty warm. As it did most Friday evenings, the mall buzzed with after-work energy. Later, it would give way to the drunken revelry of college-age kids, but for now, the crowd was slightly older, sharing a few drinks with coworkers before heading home for the weekend. The patio of the martini bar was full. Men in suits, women in skirts, one table of drinkers all wearing medical scrubs, toasting each other, laughing a bit too loud.

Two violinists were playing an impromptu concert in the small amphitheater in the center of the square. Kids splashed in the fountain while their parents lounged in the sun on the stone steps, toes tapping to the rhythm. Not only to the music from the musicians, but to the entire ensemble—the drinkers, the shoppers, the kids shouting and giggling. The strings of lights overhead were beginning to twinkle on, even though it wasn't yet dark. The bright earthy smell of the linden trees mingled with the scent of coffee and the sweet aroma of ice cream. Two men sat on a bench, kissing—not the lewd public affection so common among teenagers. It was sweeter than that. These men were a bit older, a bit more reserved. I imagined they were crazy in love.

I tried not to be jealous.

I sighed and reached into my pocket to finger the box holding Stacey's rejected present. No point in delaying the inevitable any longer.

The pawnshop was northeast of the mall, a block east of Nick's office. I found the owner sitting in exactly the same spot—feet on the counter, cigarette drooping from his mouth, magazine in his hand. He raised his eyebrows at me.

"Back already?"

"I'm afraid so." I pulled out the box and placed it on the counter. "I need to return this."

He stubbed out his cigarette and rubbed the back of his head with his other hand.

"I don't normally take returns. That's sort of counter to how pawnshops work, you know?"

No, I didn't know. I felt a blush creeping up my cheeks.

He took his feet off the counter and tossed his magazine aside. "Lucky for you, I have a soft spot for redheads."

That made me blush even more, and I automatically reached up to touch my own hair. I'd described it on my driver's license as light brown, but it wasn't the first time I'd been called a redhead.

He seemed unaware of my discomfort. He reached out and took the box, opening it to check the necklace.

"Girlfriend didn't like it?"

"It's probably more accurate to say that she doesn't like me. Not anymore."

His eyebrows went up again, and he stared at me, not as if he was unsure of what to say, but as if he had several options and was debating between them. I rubbed my forehead and wished I could take the statement back. Nothing like blurting out uncomfortable truths to total strangers. "Can I get a refund or not?"

"I'm going to do you one better than that, my friend. I'm going to buy you a drink."

The pawnshop owner had long legs and an even longer stride, and I had to hurry to keep up with him. "What's your name?" I asked as we turned the corner and headed east.

"Emanuel. But this ain't Walnut Grove, my friend, so don't even think about calling me Manny."

"Huh?"

"My friends call me El. You the kind of guy who's gonna freak out if I take you into the gay bar?"

"No." I'd never been in one, but that didn't mean I was opposed. "I don't dance, though."

He laughed. "Good. That makes two of us."

At the end of the block was Lights Out. It wasn't the only gay bar in the Light District, but it was certainly the loudest. Rainbow flags flew above the door, and the bass from dance music boomed from the building. At the door, we were greeted by a bouncer who made the Jolly Green Giant look like a sprout. He flexed arms the size of fire hydrants as he smiled at El.

"Look who got out from behind the counter, and not to do laundry." He pounded Emanuel's shoulder with a hand as big as my head. "Must have had a rough day."

"Not me. Him." Emanuel hooked a thumb in my direction.

Paul Bunyan looked back at me, first in surprise, then with obvious curiosity. He smirked and raised a questioning eyebrow at Emanuel.

"Don't even start," El said.

The big man laughed and moved aside to let us in. He didn't take his eyes off me, though. I was sure I could feel myself shrinking as I squeezed past him into the club.

It seemed like a meat market, which worried me a bit. I hadn't wanted to seem rude about being taken to a gay bar, but now that I was in one, I felt more than a little exposed. It was one thing for someone to mistake me for gay by accident—which had happened, even when Stacey and I had been out together—but to be at a gay bar seemed to invite speculation I wasn't interested in courting.

I was trying to think of an excuse to leave, but El led me up a flight of stairs before I could work up to the act. The second floor was quieter and a lot smaller, with only a few patrons visible, each of them with "local" all but stamped on their foreheads as they hunched over their drinks.

El motioned to the bartender, who came over and grinned at El, extending his hand. "Good to see you, El. What brings you out of your dusty old shop today?"

El shook his hand and gestured between us. "Paul, this is Jase, who owns this firetrap. Jase, this is Paul, who's had a very bad day."

"Pleased to meet you, Paul. What are you drinking?"

"Uh . . ." I hardly ever drank, and I had no idea what to ask for.

El waved his hand at me dismissively. "Two 90 Shillings for me, and whatever guys like him drink."

The bartender looked me up and down with an appraising eye that made me blush. "He looks like the rum and Coke type to me."

El looked me up and down too. Unlike me, he seemed completely unembarrassed. "Better make it a tall."

The bartender laughed, and the next thing I knew, I had a pint-sized glass in my hand.

"Patio open tonight?"

"For you, it's always open."

Emanuel handed him a ten-dollar tip. "Thanks, Jase."

I followed him past the bar, down a narrow hallway, past the bathrooms, through a door marked *Employees Only*, then up a dark, steep flight of stairs and through a doorway.

We emerged onto the roof of the bar. The beat of the music was still discernible, more as a vibration against the soles of my feet than a sound in my ears. The Light District spread out below us, and the bright white lights of downtown seemed perfect under the orange glow of the sunset.

There were two small round tables, each with a couple of metal patio chairs.

"The smoking ordinances in this town are almost enough to make me quit." El pulled a pack out of his shirt pocket and grinned at me as he sat down. "*Almost.*"

I sat down opposite him and watched as he lit a cigarette and slipped his lighter back into his pocket.

"So," he said as he propped one booted foot up on the table, "tell me about your girl."

I felt myself blush. Why was he asking about that? I'd only just learned his name. It seemed a bit soon to be talking about Stacey, but he was staring right at me, his expression guarded though not unfriendly. He seemed interested, and yet not in a nosey kind of way. I suspected he was older than me by a few years, though most of that came from the impression he gave of having seen everything at least once, like nothing in the world could surprise him.

"Stacey and I met in college," I said at last. "At CSU. We were only nineteen." She was the only woman I'd ever been with. In fact, other than a few nervous, fumbling, high school encounters with one of the neighbor boys, she was the only sexual partner I'd ever had at all, but I didn't feel compelled to share *that* with Emanuel.

"She's an artist. A welder. She makes these big metal sculptures, and she wanted to move here—"

"Of course she did. What artist doesn't want to move to Hacktown?"

I blinked at the derogatory nickname for the Light District, having only heard it a few times, usually from locals making fun of it. That El would be one of them surprised me, but then I realize he was disliking Stacey more than anything. I couldn't decide if that made me feel defensive for her or pleased that he was dissing my ex.

He waved his hand to send his cigarette smoke floating the other way instead of into my face. "So what happened?"

"We broke up. Two months ago."

"I take it that wasn't your idea."

"No. She left me for somebody else. He's an art professor at Tucker U."

I stopped and took a giant drink. El continued to watch me. The fading orange light from the west glowed against one side of his face and left the other side in shadow.

"I gave her everything," I said. It seemed stupid to reveal so much to him, and yet suddenly, I *had* to say it. I longed to tell somebody my side of the story—not to justify anything, but to get it out. To purge it. I'd been too embarrassed to bring it up with Nick in any kind of detail. I hadn't yet told my parents that Stacey had left me. Every other person I knew in Tucker Springs was more Stacey's friend than mine. There'd been absolutely nobody for me to talk to about it. Until now.

"Nothing was ever good enough. I planned to be a veterinarian, and she liked that. Somehow, that was respectable, I guess. I did fine in undergrad, but I failed out of vet school, and everything went downhill from that point on." Looking back, I wondered if she'd decided right then that I'd never be good enough. Maybe she hadn't even quite been aware of it herself, but I was pretty sure she'd never felt the same about me after that.

"She's one of those people who grew up playing tennis, you know? And golf at the country club. And she wants that life, but she wants to be an artist too, which means she has to marry well. And I no longer qualify. So now I'm stuck here, with eighteen months left on a lease in a house where I can't have pets. Every credit card I have is maxed out because she had to have every damn thing she ever saw. I still have student loans to pay back, which I can't help but think would be less or already taken care of if we hadn't been so busy paying for everything she wanted. And for some goddamn stupid reason I can't even explain to myself, I still want her back."

I tipped my drink back and gulped it all down. I didn't look at him. I set the glass on the table and stared at it rather than face whatever might be in his eyes. "That's why I bought the necklace."

He was quiet, but after a few seconds of contemplative silence, he took his foot off the table. For one second, I thought he was going to stand up, but he didn't. He crushed his cigarette butt out in the ashtray between us, then leaned his elbows on the table to stare at me. "You know what the root of all evil is?"

I blinked at him, trying to figure out where he was going with the question. "Money?"

"No, man. It's *stuff*. Possessions. *Things*. All that crap money buys. All the shit we tell ourselves we need. You have any idea how many people come into my shop every week and they got to trade in some gadget so they can pay the rent? The thing is, you ask them, 'Did you know rent was due?' Of course they did. 'Did you realize you didn't have another payday between now and then?' Yeah, they knew that too. 'So why'd you decide to drop five hundred on an iPad?' And they don't got an answer, and if they do, it's something ridiculous. It's new. It's hip. It's shiny. It's loud. Their neighbor has one, or their sister, or their boss, and they can't stand to let others have things they don't. They're so afraid of what others might think. Their kid is sitting there in a dirty diaper and a T-shirt two sizes too small. Thirty degrees outside and they didn't bother to put pants on the poor kid, let alone socks and a jacket, but they drove right down to Best Buy the minute it opened to buy the newest Xbox, and now they're scratching their heads wondering why they can't pay for heat.

"You fell into it, Paul. Into the mindset. Into the lie. But it's not just you. Not just Stacey, either. It's almost every other red-blooded American out there. Now you're at the end of it, and you can't beat yourself up. There's no point in punishing yourself, because it's over. The thing is, now you know the way out."

"I do?" I wasn't sure if it was the alcohol or him that had me confused.

"Yeah."

I sat there, stunned, baffled, a bit amused. I had several questions I wanted to ask, not the least of which was, *What the hell are you talking about?* What I ended up saying was, "Why are you doing this?"

"Doing what?"

"Hanging out with me. Buying me drinks."

"Is it that much of a mystery?"

"Kind of, yeah."

A ghost of a smile played over his full lips. He raised an eyebrow at me. "You're not worried about the fact that I brought you to a gay bar?"

Alarm bells went off in my head, but I chastised myself. Surely he was just teasing me. "Should I be?"

This time he really did smile, a mischievous one that caused butterflies to take flight in my chest. When was the last time somebody had bothered to flirt with me? Even as a joke?

Emanuel slid one of his two untouched beers my way. "Here," he said as he leaned back to light his next cigarette, "have another drink."

CHAPTER 4

What are you doing?

The question kept rattling around El's head as he watched his adorable, straight, hot mess of a redhead finish off his first beer and blithely accept another when offered it. El told himself he was amused, that was all. Bemused, actually, because he couldn't quite make Paul out. Which meant he was bored and feeding Paul drinks and watching what happened as a way to pass the time.

Except he watched the way Paul's lips clung to the glass and had to check urges to skim his knuckles down Paul's sharp, innocent cheekbones.

What was he doing, indeed?

"So what are you going to do?" El asked, forcing himself to stop having idiot fantasies. Maybe if Paul talked about his ex-girlfriend enough, El could write him off as another sorry sap serving as a walking advertisement for why not to have relationships. Not to mention that if they both said *girlfriend* often enough, maybe El would cotton on to the fact that Paul was straight.

Paul blinked at El in drunken confusion. "Do?"

The more clueless Paul got, the more adorable he became. "About Stacey," El prompted.

"Oh." Paul stared sadly into his half-spent glass. "Nothing, I guess."

Right. Obviously. "Moving on then? More fish in the sea?" El nodded wryly at the door throbbing with club music. "Should have taken you to your kind of pond."

Paul blinked as if he didn't understand. "Pond? Oh." His gaze returned to the glass again. El began to wonder if Paul thought it might be some kind of alcoholic gazing glass. "I don't think I have a pond."

"Oh yes. That's right, I forgot we were supposed to be picking up people at the laundromat." When Paul registered even deeper confusion, El reached for his cigarettes and lit up. "It's a joke. I told a friend of mine we shouldn't try to make hookups in bars but at regular places, and now it's kind of a running theme."

For a second, El worried Paul might think that's what this was, a hookup, but then he remembered Paul was Captain Clueless. He seemed to be considering El's theory of relationships, though, and after a few moments of drunken pensiveness, he nodded. "That's true. I met Stacey in the school commons. She needed someone to hold her books while she wiped up a coffee someone had spilled across our table, and she bought me lunch as a thank-you. Everything sort of happened from there."

It was his face, El decided, the way you could see everything he thought about as it passed between his ears. Guileless, simple thoughts. For example, right now Paul was trying to figure out how he could repeat that kind of scenario. El would've bet money on it.

Too bad he wasn't the relationship type. Too bad Paul was straight. Too bad no relationship ever worked out, period.

El wondered about Paul being entirely straight, though, like when El's conscience got the better of him and compelled him to shuttle Paul back to his house. It wasn't the fact that Paul clung to El while he held him up—he was drunk; that came with the territory. The glances, though, made El pause. Paul checking the way El filled out his T-shirt. Staring at El's waist after he'd poured Paul into bed. Simple things that were almost guaranteed to be El reading into his intentions.

Simple things, though, that fucked royally with El's head.

He stopped by Rosa's the next day and listened to her carry on about her man of the moment, listened as she spouted the same lines she always did about how they'd made a connection, about how there was something special about this one, about how she could tell by looking into his eyes that he understood her in a way no one else had. El wished he had the other seventy times she'd told him that on tape to play back to her, but it wouldn't have mattered. She'd still be convinced this was The One, right up until the moment he cheated on her or left her without warning or some new twist proved he was The Same One as Always.

She never listened because she was lonely. El knew that. As he thought about it, he realized that was his problem too, though not in the same way. He was plugging into the same bullshit, thinking someone who felt off the beaten path could work some kind of magic and fill his life with cheesy soundtracks and longing glances.

Which was crazy. El liked his life. It was the way he wanted it. He hated cheesy soundtracks, and he never glanced longingly at anything. Paul was amusing and entertaining. Adorable too, yes. And straight.

Not that any of it mattered, because El didn't do relationships, and he wasn't going to be doing Paul.

So there wasn't any harm in enjoying his company, because Paul didn't have a pond and El didn't want to go fishing.

Or something like that.

CHAPTER 5

The morning after my night with El at the bar, I woke feeling thick-headed and groggy. The beer had been a bit too dark and intense for me, much like Emanuel himself. Still, I felt better for having spent time with him. Somehow lighter for having spilled my guts to a man I barely knew. It seemed like I should feel awkward about it, but I didn't. El's simple acceptance of it all, as if it were a story he'd heard a hundred times before, made it easier. It was like having gone to confession, but without any of the Hail Marys.

My mom called early in the afternoon and asked to talk to Stacey. "I thought I'd wish her a happy birthday."

I debated lying and telling her that Stacey was out for the day, but that would only delay the inevitable. I hated to disappoint my mom, but there was really no way to avoid it any longer.

"She doesn't live here anymore, Mom."

A heartbeat of silence, then, "What do you mean?"

She knew what I meant. Her question had more to do with filling an awkward space than with needing an explanation, but I gave one anyway. "She left me."

It made me sad how Mom almost sounded relieved. "Did the two of you have a fight?"

If only it had been that simple. "She decided we were going in different directions." What that really meant was that she'd decided I couldn't give her what she wanted, but no need to be too blatant about my shortcomings. I shut my eyes, hating that I had failed like this, hated what my mother was about to think of me. "She met somebody else. A professor at the university."

"Oh, Paul. I'm so sorry. Are you doing okay?"

"I'm fine, Ma," I lied.

"You're such a nice boy, honey. You'll meet somebody else. I know you will. Somebody who truly appreciates you."

Leave it to my mom to pull out the most clichéd mother speech ever. And yet, it helped a bit. "From your lips to God's ears."

"How's the clinic?"

"Fine."

"Do you still like it?"

"I do. My boss is a great guy, and I love all the animals, you know?" I wished I hadn't disappointed everybody by failing so miserably, though. I should have been the veterinarian. Instead, I answered the phone for Nick and sent out bills.

No girlfriend. No fiancée. No real job. No real life. Just some secondhand makeshift number I'd pulled out of the wreckage of what should have been.

Mom interrupted my pity party with a depressingly upbeat tone that screamed Bright New Idea. "Do you have any plans for the summer?"

"Not really. I can't afford to go anywhere." I could barely afford to stay put, either, but that made me think about the pink flier. "My neighborhood is having this contest for nice yards. The prize is $500."

"That sounds like a good way to get outside," she said. "Get some sun. Maybe you'll meet someone nice."

"In my front lawn?"

"Stranger things have happened."

I laughed. My mother was an optimist and a hopeless romantic. She called me a pessimist, but I didn't see it that way. I dwelt closer to the land of reality. "I'll settle for the cash prize, but thanks anyway."

"I'm thinking about coming to visit you in a couple of weeks. Your dad's busy, but I could come."

I found myself smiling. "There's not really that much to see here."

"You're there, honey. That's enough for me."

I started on the yard that day. Mowing was easy, but there was tall grass around the base of Stacey's sculptures that I couldn't get to with the mower, and bushes and abandoned flower beds all around the base of the house. I pulled plants that I hoped were weeds and left ones that I hoped weren't. It immediately became apparent that the mower and my hands were insufficient tools.

I went into the detached garage. It had been set up as Stacey's studio, and a few pieces of scrap metal still lay on the floor. I could have put my car in the garage if I'd put a bit of effort into it, but so far, it hadn't been necessary. I'd probably want to deal with it before winter came, though.

We'd lived in an apartment building back in Fort Collins and so hadn't ever needed landscaping tools, but that was the type of thing tenants sometimes left behind, so I checked the corners of the garage. I did find the snow shovel that had died from the previous year's epic snow, a plastic rake that was missing more tines than not, and one very rusty hoe, but that was it.

I got in my car, intending to hit the nearest hardware store, but El's flashing "BUY - SELL - PAWN" sign caught my eye, and I looped around the block to find a parking space. I had no idea if people pawned gardening tools, but I figured it couldn't hurt to try.

El was right where he'd been the last two times I'd been in the shop, reading a magazine with his feet up on the counter. He smiled at me and stood up as I came in.

"Tell me you're not here to buy more jewelry for your girl."

I tried to smile back, although it was harder than I would have liked. "No jewelry," I said. "I'm actually looking for yard things."

"'Things'? We talking 'things' like gnomes and plastic Bambis?"

"I was thinking a little less tacky and a bit more utilitarian."

He laughed. "Fair enough. What'd you have in mind?"

"I need one of those spinny weed-chopping things."

He rubbed the short hair at the nape of his neck. "It so happens I have not one, but *two* of those 'spinny weed-chopping things.'" He gestured toward the back corner of the shop. "You want gas-powered or electric?"

I hadn't realized there were different types. "Whichever's cheapest, I guess."

He seemed to find that funny. He smiled and touched the rectangular bulge in his shirt pocket but didn't pull the cigarettes out. "Not exactly aiming to make yourself my favorite customer, are you?" The way he said it wasn't mean, though. His tone was light.

"Don't take it personally," I said. "I'm broke."

He laughed. "You and everybody else who walks through that door."

Twenty minutes later, I was home with my electric weed whacker. My neighbor Bill, a man only a few years older than me but missing most of his hair, stood watering his front yard by hand. I tried to look like I actually knew what I was doing with the tool and prayed I wouldn't make a total fool of myself by chopping my own foot off.

The outlet in the garage didn't work, but after hunting around in the bushes, I found one near the front porch that did, and after only a few minutes, I'd successfully spin-chopped the tall grass around Stacey's sculptures and all along the base of the house. Unfortunately, when I stood back and examined my work, my heart sank. The grasses and weeds had been overgrown, but with them gone, the cement foundation of the house was left exposed. The barren flowerbeds looked even more pitiful than before.

"You should plant some flowers."

I turned around to find a cartoon character come to life. A young woman who could have been Velma from the old *Scooby-Doo* shows was standing behind me, using her hand to block the sun from her spectacled eyes.

"Excuse me?" I asked.

"Irises would be perfect, but it's not the right time of year. Maybe something tall like lilies or columbines. Sunflowers are nice, too."

Flowers would help hide the gray foundation of the house, and the flier had said the judges would be on the lookout for yards that were well-kept, colorful, and inviting. Of course, flowers would also cost money. How much could I justify spending in an effort to win $500?

I glanced over at my neighbor, who stood watching me, his hose hanging forgotten in his hand. He was clearly hoping to win the money, too.

"That's a good idea," I said to Velma. "Thanks for the advice."

She smiled at me. "You bet."

Too bad the pawnshop didn't sell flowers.

CHAPTER 6

"So," Denver said as he shoved his laundry into the washing machine next to El, "what's up with Strawberry Shortcake?"

El laughed, less at Denver's description of Paul than at the fact that El knew exactly who his friend meant. "Nothing."

"Not like you to date, is it? Always thought you were more about quick and easy."

"It wasn't a date."

"It looked like one."

Choosing not to answer, El finished loading the washer and put his money in.

"Not sure what I thought your type was," Denver said, "but that skinny kid sure wasn't it."

His words annoyed El, but the fact that he was annoyed at all annoyed him even more. "Lay off, man."

Denver leaned against his machine. "Don't get touchy. Kinda got a thing for that type myself. Just not what I imagined you being into, that's all."

"That's because I'm not," El said, but there wasn't much conviction behind it.

El couldn't really say that he'd ever had a "type" the way Denver meant it. For him, real attraction had never been about age or size or the color of their hair. It was more complicated than that. It had to do with gentleness and vulnerability, and the truth was, Paul had both those things in spades. He was the only thing El had thought about for days. Something about his confused eyes and his freckled nose made El smile. The thought of his pale lips and the soft skin of his throat made El's heart pound and his blood race for his groin.

"You're smiling," Denver said, interrupting El's thoughts. "Cut it out. You're giving me the creeps."

"It's not that unusual, is it?" El asked as they headed for the booth to wait out the wash cycle.

"It's not that you're smiling. It's the way you're doing it."

That brought El up short. "What the fuck's that mean?"

Denver sat down and regarded him across the mustard-yellow Formica of the table. "Nothing wrong with admitting you like him, you know."

"I have an idea." El turned to stretch his legs out along the length of the plastic bench. "Let's talk about *your* love life."

Instead of answering, Denver flipped him the bird. Which was exactly what El had expected. Denver Rogers was not the kind of guy who sat around laundromats chatting about his personal life.

"Fine," Denver conceded. "Forget Strawberry Shortcake. Tell me the latest about your sister."

"She's in love. He's wonderful. He's the best thing that ever happened to her. For now." El's fingers itched for a cigarette but had to settle for drumming irritably against his thigh. "This one isn't an ass to the kids, which is a nice change."

"Maybe it will work out this time."

El couldn't decide if Denver was deliberately trying to rile him up or if he truly was that secretly romantic. With Denver, one never really knew. Threading his hands behind his neck, El regarded Denver. "So what about you? When you moved to town four months ago, you said you were passing through. You look like you're settling in."

Denver shrugged noncommittally. "Maybe. Jase's still paying me, and I got plenty of ass on tap. What more is there?"

They'd had this conversation before, and El always got some version of that answer. Except it wasn't entirely unlike watching Paul and thinking there was something more there, something that hadn't woken up yet. Denver wasn't exactly Sleeping Beauty. El did think, though, that he was looking for something, waiting for something.

Which was pretty normal. Everybody was, and nobody was ever going to find it.

"What there is, Mr. Rogers, is ten more minutes on my spin cycle, and I'm going to spend them smoking a cigarette. Care to join me?"

"Nah. I'll just sit here and hope Mr. Right stumbles into my arms."

El patted him on the shoulder as he rose. "Good luck with that."

CHAPTER 7

I went to a couple of local nurseries on Sunday in search of plants. After returning the necklace, I had a bit of cash, and I bought a few canisters of lilies and hostas. It seemed like a lot of plants until I got home and lined them up in front of my house. I had hoped to hide the cement foundation of the house, but the plants I had were barely enough to fill the gap next to the front porch.

Of course my next dilemma was how to plant them. The only shovel I owned was made for shoveling snow, not digging holes. I wondered if El had shovels at his shop and whether or not he was open on Sundays. Next door, Bill was using some kind of tool that looked like a spur on a stick to trim the edges of his lawn where the grass met the sidewalk. I considered asking him for a shovel, but it seemed a bit wrong to ask the competition for help. In the end, I drove to the hardware store and spent my last bit of cash on a shovel.

By the time I went to bed on Sunday, I was sunburned and sore, but the flowers were happily settled into the corner by the porch. They looked better than I'd expected them to.

Monday turned out to be a good day at the office. Nick's veterinary technician, Brooke, called in sick, and on the third patient of the day, Nick asked me to help him examine a nervous shepherd mix named Samson.

"He's a stray," Nick said. "Going up for adoption soon, hopefully." Nick did free exams for the local Humane Society, and we had several animals a week who had to be cleared physically before they could enter the adoption program. "He seems friendly enough, but he's obviously scared to death, so I'd rather have some help. Do you know how to hold him?"

"Of course." I remembered that much from veterinary school, at least. I wrapped one arm around him to hold his legs, and used my other arm to pull him tight against me, with my hand around his muzzle in case he tried to bite. I talked quietly to him while Nick checked him. "Such a good boy. You're a good boy. Such a pretty dog, going to find a forever home soon, aren't you? Because you're so good, not fighting while the nice doctor checks you out." Nick rolled his eyes at me, and I couldn't exactly blame him, but Samson settled in against me, and his trembling eased a bit. I kept up my inane drone of words while Nick did the exam.

"Good, good boy. We have treats for good dogs, too. Then you'll go find a home, won't you?"

Samson passed the exam with flying colors, and I hoped he really would find a home soon.

I helped with several examinations that morning: a Chesapeake Bay Retriever, a surly gray rabbit, and two cats.

"You're good at this," Nick said at lunchtime. "You have a real knack with the animals."

"I always have," I admitted. "That's why I went to vet school." Too bad I hadn't been able to finish.

After lunch, one of Nick's regular clients came in with an entire litter of puppies to be checked. Nick didn't necessarily need help with puppies, but there were six of them, and wrangling them gave me a perfectly good excuse to pet them all, and nuzzle them, and blow gently so they'd flap their tongues toward my face.

"There's no better smell in the world than puppy breath," I said to Nick.

He laughed. "True enough. It'll cure what ails you."

I spent so much time helping Nick that half of my regular work didn't get done. "Do you want me to stay late?"

"Your call. Stay, if you'd rather do it today, but there's nothing there that won't keep overnight."

Yes, it would be a bit more work the next day, but it had been worth it. Working in the exam room with him had cheered me up. I was in a good mood until I pulled up in front of my house. Bill was nowhere to be seen, but across the front of his house, where the day before there had been only grass, stretched a long line of rose bushes. Leafy and beautiful and so fragrant I could smell them when I got out of my car.

"Son of a bitch," I mumbled. "He would have to buy flowers, too."

The next day at work, I was pleased when Brooke called in sick for the second day in a row. I knew it was a bit sadistic of me to be happy about her having the flu, but I was thrilled to have a second day helping with the animals. I rushed to get my other work done in between the times Nick needed me. It was draining, but worth it. I was more than a little disappointed when Brooke showed up for work on Wednesday and I had to go back to answering the phone and shuffling papers.

Bill's lawn was looking better than ever, which annoyed me to no end. I eyed the rest of the houses on my street. I wasn't sure if they looked any different than they had last week or not, and of course there were two more blocks of houses in our neighborhood I couldn't see from my own yard.

On Thursday, I logged into the Curb Appeal site. Houses in the neighborhood were rated one through ten, ten being the ideal, and one meaning burnt couches and rusty cars on cinderblocks in the front yard. Nobody had tens yet, presumably to give everybody incentive. In fact, the highest rating in the entire neighborhood was an eight, somewhere on the next block over. There were a few sevens. Bill was one of them.

I rated a six.

There was still plenty of time for me to win. But where would I get the money?

I spent the last half of the week worrying over my bills. Between credit cards, student loans, rent, and utilities, my finances were a disaster. I could pay everything, but with very little to spare for non-essentials. My mind kept returning to the Curb Appeal contest. Five hundred dollars would come in handy, but in order to beat Bill, I'd need to invest what little cash I had left in more flowers. Was it worth it? I wasn't sure.

One night I wandered into my pantry, looking for dinner. The light switch was fussy, and it took me several tries to get the lights to stay on. Fiddling with it reminded me of how Stacey hadn't ever been able to get it wiggled into the mysterious halfway point where the connection would take, of how I always had to do it for her. It was probably one of the few real assets I'd brought to our relationship.

Larry's house had great wiring and no trick light switches. I was sure of it.

Dodgy wiring aside, the real issue on my mind that night was food. I wouldn't be able to go grocery shopping until after payday, so I had to make do with whatever I had. Sadly, what I had wasn't much. A box of Rice Krispies and one of Cheerios. Some stale hotdog buns. Half a box of Girl Scout cookies. A package of Ramen and three cans of tomato soup. The rest of the pantry was taken up by small appliances. A George Foreman Grill, a waffle maker, a cappuccino machine, a bread maker, a food processor with a billion attachments, a wok, and a turkey fryer. A rice cooker and two different crockpots. A panini press, a funky little hand-blender that confounded me, and a fondue pot we'd used exactly once. They were all things Stacey had insisted we needed at one time or another in our six and a half years together. I'd bought them for her because I'd wanted to give her the life I thought she wanted. I'd wanted to prove I could be what she needed.

Somehow, they'd all been status symbols, and yet, how could any of it matter if nobody knew about them anyway? What good did they do us?

How often had she used any of them?

I thought about the things Emanuel had said about possessions. *Stuff*. Now it was nothing more than wasted money on a shelf.

But I had a plan.

CHAPTER 8

O n Saturday, El's family reminded him why his fondest wish through junior high and high school had been to become an orphan.

Everything with his family was a battle. Family gatherings were not quiet idylls on the back patio sipping beer while the kids ran in circles after a couple of dogs. In fact, usually the Rozals looked like the highlight reel from a documentary film about troubled families right before the film crew gave in and called the cops. Someone shouted while someone else cried quietly in the corner, and the doors always slammed. The kids usually did a kind of warm-up to the adults' drama, fighting over who had brought what toy and how long they'd played with it and whether or not it had been broken before they had it. The adults argued over who had done what family chore or drunk the last beer. Even if El managed to stay out of the opening act, he'd be dragged into it eventually as someone's unwilling ally, at which point he'd have to say he did or didn't agree, immediately putting himself on a side. He couldn't even walk out, because Uncle Mariano would follow and read him the riot act for disrespecting family. El's defense for dealing with his relatives had been to be so "busy" with work he couldn't come.

When Abuela called and told El she needed help moving some things from the attic, however, El didn't have a choice. He couldn't say no to his grandmother, and she knew it. After closing the shop early and bracing himself for a long, grueling afternoon, El coached himself for the reality that he'd likely leave the house frustrated and angry. He warned himself not to engage, to let everything roll off his back, and under no circumstances to get embroiled in the drama.

He rounded the corner of his grandmother's street, saw the pile of crap teetering near the edge of the front porch, and plugged in so hard and deep it was like he'd never left.

While he'd known his mom's hoard would be worse because it always was, and because it had been three months since he'd last been over, the reality of what she'd done to Abuela's house hit El the same way it always did: as a bitter cocktail of frustration, fear, and loss. The porch swing, where he'd sat joking with the neighbor boy, had snapped and broken beneath the weight of plastic bins, broken yard tools, and God knew what else. Junk. Shit that should have gone out with the trash years ago. Not to his mom, though. Nothing was ever trash to Patricia Rozal.

She met El at the door, embracing him like the prodigal son, smelling like tortillas and cinnamon. "Emanuel, so good to see you." She kissed him hard on the cheek and pulled him by the hand deeper into the house. "*Mami, Emanuel ya está aquí.*"

The path to the kitchen was as circuitous as ever, taking them around the dining room table—piled two feet high with paper and boxes—around a precariously stacked mess of Rubbermaid bins, and through a tunnel of hanging clothes clogging the doorway. The kitchen itself was mostly okay, because that was Abuela's domain, but El couldn't help noticing the piles of mail and the latest shopping on the table.

He smiled and hugged his grandmother, accepting her kisses as she fussed in Spanish, telling him he was too thin and smelled like smoke.

Though he could hear the telltale shrieks of Rosa's eldest drifting in through the window, Rosa wasn't there, which was a blessing because Lorenzo's wife Anna was, and as far as El knew, she and Rosa were still fighting. Anna sat at the table with Sary, Miguel's wife, and Sary's eldest daughter, Lila, the three of them filling tamales. They'd broken up the tasks, Lila drying the husks, Anna pressing out the masa, and Sary adding the meat and rolling the whole thing up and adding it to the pan of items waiting to be steamed.

Anna smiled and waved at him, looking weary. "How's it going, El?"

"Good." He moved junk from a chair and sat down between her and Lila. "What about you?"

El listened as they took turns talking about work, school, and kids. Lila rolled her eyes a lot and played the part of a disinterested pre-teen, abandoning her assigned task of drying the soaked husks to check her constant stream of text messages. Sary asked about the shop, poking El for funny stories about things people tried to sell, and he told her a couple.

When Patti started to inventory her latest Goodwill purchases, though, El left the table and went to Abuela at the stove.

"Smells good." He tried to sneak a bite of beans from the back burner, and smiled when she smacked his hand and waved a finger at him.

"I know your tricks. No fingers in my pot." She smiled, though, and turned toward El as she worked. "Thank you for coming, *mijo*. I miss you when you stay away too long."

El missed her too. But admitting that would open up the old argument about his mom, so he didn't go there. He pointed to the pan of beans in front of him, instead. "Can I stir this for you?"

"*Sí*. You stir, we talk." She handed him a spatula. "So. Emanuel. You meet a nice boy?" He tried to laugh her question off, but Paul's face drifted into his head. El became very busy stirring the beans, but there was never any getting past Abuela. She sighed happily and patted him on the shoulder. "You ask him out, *sí?* You bring him to your Abuela. I make him tamales."

He didn't argue because it would only make things worse. Besides, he was distracted by the mental image of Paul tasting his grandmother's food, face lighting up in joy.

Of course, the fact that it would happen in his mother's hoard cooled the image pretty quickly.

"I don't have anyone to ask out," El told her. "Don't worry about me, Abuela. I'm fine."

She clucked her tongue and touched his hair. "You are lonely, Emanuel. You need nice boy to make you happy."

"I am happy."

She made a face and waved his idea away. "You sit in pawnshop and smoke cigarettes all day. That is not happiness."

"Abuela," El complained.

"You hide from life. You have no joy, no family, no passion. You sell other people's things and get cancer and break my heart."

"*Abuela*." He stopped stirring and reached for her arm, but she moved it away to wipe tears from her eyes. Before he could figure out what to say, she recovered, patting his hand as she took the spatula back.

"Let me cook. You go talk with your brothers. Go," she added, when he tried to protest.

With little left to do, El kissed her on the cheek and went outside.

Lorenzo and Miguel stood with Uncle Mariano on the back porch, sipping beer and watching the kids run around the yard. They nodded and greeted El as he approached. The kids were crazy loud, cutting off any chance for real conversation, though Lorenzo and Miguel had long since become immune to the noise. Adding to the chaos was occasional static from Miguel's radio, which meant he was on call for the volunteer fire department.

"What are we moving down from the attic?" El asked his uncle.

The grim look on his face didn't bode well. "Mami wants to try and get rid of a few of Papi's things."

El wished he'd grabbed a beer from the fridge. Hell, he wished he'd snagged a bottle of vodka. "Shit."

Uncle Mariano held up a hand. "That's why the girls are here. They're going to take Patti shopping while we work. Mami thought maybe you could take some of the things right to your shop so she wouldn't even see."

He was going to need *two* bottles of vodka. "That's the first place she's going to look."

"I know." Mariano sighed and handed over his beer. "I know."

Cleaning out the attic didn't bother El. In fact, it made him feel good, even though he was sure he'd never been dirtier in his life. What upset him wasn't the work or what they removed to sell or junk. What upset him were the things they left behind.

He understood his mom was sick, that hoarding was a psychological condition, that it had more to do with unresolved loss and other head-shrinky things than with crass commercialism and sentimentality. On a purely academic level, he even empathized. Reality, though, was difficult to swallow. Reality was slipping on papers that littered the stairs as he helped Lorenzo haul Abuelo's old tools out to his truck, knowing they had to move fast because if Patti came back before they were done, they were screwed, that the fit to end all fits would ensue. Reality was standing in the sweltering heat of the attic with dust choking their throats as they argued over how much they could take before she'd miss anything. Reality was knowing the piece-of-junk eight-track player they found wouldn't bring ten bucks in El's shop but would send his mother into spirals of betrayal, so they couldn't even throw it out.

Reality was hauling only three pickup-loads worth of stuff out of the attic and leaving a house full of crap behind.

They managed to pull it off, though, and by the time the girls got back, the men had returned to the patio with a fresh round of beer and huge plates of food. They kept quiet, knowing it wasn't over yet, that if they'd disturbed too much on the way out the door she would suspect what had been done. El thought for sure she'd figure it out because they almost never got him to come over unless it was for something like this, and he was ready for the fallout, ready despite his earlier vows to stay out of things, ready to tell his mother she had to let go, that things were only *things* and didn't matter, that it was more important her grandchildren had room to play in the house than it was for her to collect every salvageable piece of junk from people's trash. He was ready, but it never happened. She was too busy showing off the new things she'd bought, the delight and wonder they provided her dancing in her eyes.

El finished his food as quickly as he could, downed his beer, and chain-smoked his way back to his apartment over the shop.

He lay awake thinking about what Abuela had said about being lonely. There in the dark, he admitted she was right, but the truth—the cold, hard truth—was that there wasn't any sure way to happiness, or any way at all, period. Not lasting. Rosa chased men and had their babies. Patti bought crap and combed through garbage. Abuela fussed over people. Denver fucked twinks and bench-pressed cars. Jase fought to keep his bar from the bill collectors.

Nobody was happy, not really. Everyone was lonely. El and everybody else, they all waded through the misery that was life and tried to find some pleasure secondhand. Pick something at random and cling to that, because there was no magic bullet train to happiness.

That should have been enough, that talking-to he gave himself. Except damned if he didn't lie there thinking about the way Paul's hands had moved when he'd tried to mimic the motion of a weed whacker, Paul's voice echoing inside El's head, bright and polite and funny as he said over and over, "Spinny-things."

CHAPTER 9

I felt a little silly carrying a cappuccino maker into El's store, but I made myself do it anyway.

"Paul," he said when I walked in. His bright smile made me feel a little less ridiculous. "What are you doing here?"

"You give people money for stuff like this, right?" I asked as I put the machine down on the counter.

"That is part of my job description. How's the weed whacker?"

"It's good."

"And the job?"

I fidgeted, flustered by the questions. "Good, I guess." He seemed to be waiting for something, so I said, "How are you?"

His smile got bigger. "Can't complain. My day just got significantly better."

"Because you need a cappuccino maker?"

He laughed. "Yeah, that's it," he said in a way that told me that wasn't it at all.

I felt awkward, like I was missing a joke. I decided that meant I should get down to business. "So, can you give me money for this?"

He shrugged and finally bent to look at it. "Probably," he said. "I've never taken one of these before, so you might have to give me a few minutes to do some research. You want to hock it or sell it?"

"Uh . . ." I felt myself blushing. I wished he didn't always make me feel so clueless. "What's the difference?"

"Well, are you looking for a loan, hoping to buy it back later?"

"I don't ever need it back."

"In that case, I can buy it from you outright."

"I have more, too."

"More cappuccino machines?"

"No, but more kitchen stuff. Mixers and bread makers and grills. Should I go get them?"

"Are they in your car?"

"No. They're at home."

He stared at me, as if debating something. A slow smile spread across his face. "I can only take one item a day," he said, shrugging. "It's some kind of law."

That was unfortunate. It would have been better to have the money in one chunk rather than spread out over a couple of weeks, but it seemed it couldn't be helped.

"So you'll take this today, and I can bring the rest of the stuff, as long as it's only one thing per day?"

His smile grew. "Exactly."

The amount he was able to give me for the cappuccino maker was depressingly small, but it was better than nothing, and if he paid me the same amount for the rest of the junk in my pantry, I'd be doing well. I took in the panini press the next day, and the waffle maker the day after that. I took the money to the nursery and bought more flowers, and spent the weekend working on my yard.

Unfortunately, my neighbor Bill had the same idea.

His rose bushes were in full bloom, and next to them, my string of lilies and bargain bin hostas seemed pathetic. He stood in his front lawn, a sheen of sweat on his bald head, wielding a pair of red-handled clippers. I wasn't exactly sure what he was trimming. I bent my head back to my own work, trying to dig dandelions out of the dirt at the base of Stacey's chicken statue.

"It's looking great." The voice came from behind me, and I turned to find Velma. She had a sun visor on today, and a tennis skirt that revealed tan, shapely legs. "The flowers really add a lot of color, don't they?"

"Yeah, they were a good idea. Thanks for suggesting it."

She smiled at me. She had freckles on her nose. I wondered if she had a dog at home named Scooby. "You should think about some morning glories for over there." She pointed to the corner of the house. "Put a little trellis there for them to climb. Or maybe some clematis."

That corner of the yard did look bare. I'd already spent my money from El, but there were still appliances in my pantry. "Are those expensive?"

She shrugged. "I don't know. I think it would be a nice touch, though. It might make the place more inviting."

Inviting?

Was she one of the judges? I wanted to ask, but she probably wouldn't have told me anyway. I glanced over at Bill. He was at the nearest edge of his lawn, allegedly trimming something from one of his rosebushes, but I was positive he was listening in.

I turned my back on him, stepping closer to her and lowering my voice. "Which ones would be more colorful?"

She lowered her voice too. "The clematis. There are some lovely purples that grow well here."

I nodded, already debating which of Stacey's abandoned appliances would net me the most money at El's shop. "Thanks for the advice."

She waved and went on her way.

I tried to ignore the weight of Bill's angry glare between my shoulder blades.

CHAPTER 10

"**Y**ou still have a spring in your step," Denver observed the next time he and El did laundry. "I take it this means Strawberry is still in the picture?"

El took great pains to focus on matching up his socks on the folding table. "You know, you don't have to limit yourself to giving me an imaginary love life. You can make one up for yourself just as easily."

"Nah. Isn't half as fun." Denver grinned as he leaned back against the plastic row of seating, his huge arms taking up the backs of a chair in each direction. "You still stuck at flirting, or have you dusted off that box of condoms in the back of your medicine cabinet?"

El flipped him off without looking up and reached for the next sock.

He laughed and settled deeper into the row of chairs, making them groan. "You should bring him by the club tomorrow night. I'm working. I could comfort him when you don't put out."

Finishing with his socks, El moved on to underwear. "Give it a rest. He's straight."

"My ass he's straight."

"Did you miss the part where I met him while he was buying a necklace for his girlfriend?"

"Ex-girlfriend, as I recall. And it wasn't her I heard he was smiling at drunkenly across a patio table. He's also still coming in to buy things from you, unless you've crawled out from beneath the used toasters to meet him in the real world."

"He's not buying, he's selling," El corrected, then paused as he realized his mistake.

Denver's grin was feral. "I bet he's selling."

El tossed a pair of socks at his head. "Appliances, dumbass. Cappuccino makers. Blenders."

"Kitchen crap, which you bitch all to hell about taking because they never move. Interesting." He frowned. "You said he's selling like he's still doing it. How many appliances does this kid have? He sure doesn't look like someone who'd be fencing."

Shit. "I think my dryer is about done," El murmured and hurried away.

Denver didn't follow, but he didn't need to, his voice booming over the noise of the spin cycles. "Avoidance. This must be damn good, whatever it is."

A student trying to study at a table near the vending machines glared at El, likely because he didn't dare glare at someone as imposing as Denver. El staked out a spot in front of his dryer, which still had ten minutes to go.

"You know," Denver called out, "I think I have some extra crap in my closet I'm going to have to bring in sometime for you to sell."

"People are trying to work in here, you know," El shouted back at him, gesturing to the student.

Denver made a big show of stretching. "Yeah. I'll be by on Monday with lunch. We can hang out all afternoon and see who shows up."

Fuck. Crossing back to Denver's side of the laundromat, El tried to quell him with a glare, which only made him laugh. "Fine. He comes by every day to sell something. Are you happy now?"

"Giddy. El and Strawberry, sittin' in a tree."

"*He is straight.*"

"And thinking about acquiring a few angles, if he's emptying out his house to get your attention. *Interesting.*"

It would only get worse if El admitted the reason Paul kept coming was because he'd told him he could only sell one thing a day. El would have sold it as a joke about how gullible and cute Paul was, which was what he'd told himself, except he knew Denver would never buy it.

El was starting to wonder why he had.

CHAPTER 11

B y Saturday, I had clematis planted against the corner of the house and a bit more pantry space for food I didn't have. Velma appeared as I was weed-whacking around the base of Stacey's sculptures.

"It's gorgeous." Today's tennis skirt was bright turquoise. A matching headband held her auburn hair off her face. "Just wait until they start to climb the trellis. They'll be perfect."

I glanced over at Bill, who was once again standing in his front yard, water hose in hand, glaring at me. Once more I wondered if Velma was a judge for the Curb Appeal contest. If I won after taking her advice, would Bill be able to protest the decision?

Was I entirely too worried about something so silly?

Yes. Yes, I was.

Velma left, and I finished my weeding before heading back inside for a break. I was settling down on the couch with a huge bowl of pistachio ice cream when Stacey appeared. It was strange to see her walk through the front door as if nothing had changed. As if she still lived in the house. Her platinum hair was disheveled and there were smudges under her eyes. The small red birthmark high on her left cheek told me she had been crying. For some reason, it always became more prominent then.

"Stacey." I stood up. "What are you doing here?"

She shrugged and smiled at me awkwardly. "I thought I'd stop by and see how you're doing."

That was a lie. Something had obviously upset her, but confronting her about it wouldn't do me any good. I had no idea what to say. What came out was, "Would you like some ice cream?"

She laughed, a sudden bright sound that took me back to our time together and made my heart ache. "Sure. Why not?"

My hands shook as I went into the kitchen and scooped some into a bowl for her. I wished I had another flavor on hand. She didn't like pistachio. She would have preferred mint chocolate chip. She wrinkled her nose a bit when I handed her the bowl, but she smiled. "I've never understood the appeal of ice cream flavored like a nut."

"Vanilla's a nut. So's chocolate, isn't it?"

She shook her head. "No, they aren't nuts, not at all. One's an orchid and the other is a bean."

They were? This was news to me. I felt foolish, though mostly frustrated. She'd completely missed my point, except now I couldn't figure out how to articulate my point anymore. So I didn't say anything. She sat on one end of the couch and I sat on the other, my stomach in knots. I couldn't believe she was here. I tried not to wonder what it meant.

I looked at my own bowl of ice cream. I wasn't even sure I still wanted it.

"Why don't we watch a movie?" she asked.

"*Steel Magnolias*?" I hated that movie, but she loved it.

"I don't want to cry. How about something scary?"

I looked through the movie cabinet. She'd taken most everything with her when she left, but I didn't comment on that. There wasn't really anything scary left, so we settled on *Terminator 2*. I put it in the DVD player and sat back down on the couch. She immediately came closer, not quite cuddling up against me. Should I put my arm around her? Could I hold her hand? Not since our days of dating had I been so unsure around her. I held perfectly still. I kept my hands to myself.

Halfway through the movie, she scooted even closer. She leaned her head on my shoulder in a way that was heartbreakingly familiar. She put her hand on my thigh.

"I've missed you, Paul," she said quietly. "I'm so sorry about how things have gone."

"I've missed you too."

She snuggled closer, and I put my arm around her. "Did something happen?"

She went stiff and still for a moment, but then she sighed. "I don't want to talk about it."

"Are you here to stay?"

"I don't know." She settled more comfortably against me. Her hand moved higher on my thigh. "I just thought it might be nice to see you. I don't think I realized how much I missed you until now."

I rubbed her shoulder. I tried not to react to the hand on my thigh.

"It's really nice to be here," she said.

I tried to sort out what I was feeling. She was here, telling me she missed me, and yet it didn't fill me with joy or hope the way I might have expected. There was a fleeting sense of comfort. Of knowing how things would be between us. Of knowing which direction my future lay.

There was also the very real possibility of getting laid, and as shallow as it may have been, I couldn't help thinking about it.

She suddenly took her hand away from my thigh. She wrapped her arm around my waist. "Can I stay here tonight?"

My heart skipped a beat. Inside my pants, fun things began to happen.

In my head, the chipmunk quivered with anticipation. *Normal. She's here, and you can be normal again.*

And get laid.

"Sure," I said. My voice came out a bit too high and shaky. "That might be nice."

"I don't want anything to happen," she said. "I'd just like to stay and have you hold me."

"Oh." That certainly wouldn't have been my first choice, but it didn't seem like an opportune time to argue. The chipmunk agreed, undeterred by the lack of sex. I told myself to be happy with what she was giving me. Maybe this was the first step. Maybe tomorrow, we'd talk. And then she'd move home, and we'd be together again.

I'd have my life back.

I put my arms more tightly around her and bent to smell her hair. She didn't smell the same, but it was still pleasant to feel her there against me. I wondered if she'd let her hair go back to its natural color.

The movie ended. Would it be appropriate to suggest we go to bed? She'd asked to spend the night. Did she mean on the couch?

After the movie, she followed me into the bedroom. She took one of my T-shirts out of my drawer and wore it as a nightgown, as she'd always done. She climbed into bed and rested her head on my shoulder.

On my bedside table, the engagement ring I'd given her two years ago sat in a small glass dish. It had been there since she'd left. I'd spent as much on it as I'd dared, and yet it'd still seemed to disappoint her. It was nothing like the huge rocks so many of her friends wore. Maybe I could trade it in for a bigger stone.

I was still thinking about it when I fell asleep.

I woke to a muffled voice.

Stacey's voice.

I rolled over and stretched. Her side of the bed was empty, and I could hear her talking to somebody in the other room. I pulled on a pair of sweats, glancing at my bedside table as I did. The ring was still there.

How soon could I expect her to put it back on?

I found her at the kitchen table. She was still wearing nothing but her panties and my T-shirt. She had her cell phone tucked against her ear. She glanced up at me as I came in, her expression guarded.

"I have to go," she said to whoever was on the other end of the line. She put the phone down. She tried to tuck her hair behind her ears—a nervous habit she'd always had—but now it was too short and fell back in her face. She was very carefully not meeting my eyes.

"What's going on?" I asked.

She cleared her throat. She tried to push her hair behind her ears again, and when that didn't work, she held it there with her fingertips, as if staving off a headache. "Paul," she said, finally looking at me, "I'm so glad you let me stay last night."

"Of course. I mean, I'm glad you're here." I sat down across from her. She folded her hands in front of her on the table. I reached across to take one of them, but she pulled away.

"I have to go," she said. "That was Larry."

My heart began to sink. I pulled my hands back and crossed my arms over my chest. "Does he know you spent the night here?"

She pursed her lips at me. "Don't say it that way. You make it sound tawdry and cheap."

"I notice you didn't answer my question."

She shook her head. "No, he doesn't know. And he doesn't need to. I told him I was with a friend. Which is true, right?" She smiled hesitantly at me. "We're friends?"

I sighed. "You told me you missed me."

"I do," she said, a bit too quickly. "Larry and I had a fight, but I talked to him and it was really a misunderstanding—"

"So you show up here and feed me lines about how much you missed me, but now you're going to run back to him?"

"I wasn't feeding you lines, Paul. I meant what I said."

"Then why are you leaving again? If you miss me, then come home."

She shook her head. "It's not that easy."

"Bullshit."

She ignored me. "He wants to talk, and I owe it to him to hear him out."

"And move back in with him?"

"I never moved out."

That stung, all the more so because it was the truth.

"So you're not coming back home?"

"I don't know. Maybe. I have to talk to him first."

"What the fuck does that mean, Stacey? You have to get his permission?"

"It's not like that. But if I can work things out with him . . ."

"And if you can't?"

She smiled awkwardly. "Then yes, I'll come home."

I ducked my head and thought about that. It was what I'd wanted since she'd left, and yet, it wasn't. I'd wanted her to come back because she missed me. Because she loved me. But here she was, telling me that Larry was her first choice.

I was nothing more than a backup plan. Second choice again.

"Paul?"

"I'm going to be late for work," I said, which was stupid because it was Sunday.

I didn't bother waiting for a response. I went in the bathroom and took the hottest shower I could stand. It felt like penance. Punishment for having been a fool.

When I came back out, she was gone.

I stood there for a long time, wrapped in a towel as my hair dripped onto my shoulders, the strangeness of the evening and the night and the morning and, well, everything swirling around me. Stacey had come back. Stacey was gone again. Stacey had gone back to Larry.

I should have been upset. I should have felt devastated.

I felt . . . tired.

Without consciously making a decision to do so, I got dressed, grabbed my keys and my wallet, and started walking. After a block I realized I'd forgotten my phone, but I decided I didn't care. What did I need a phone for? Who did I think I'd call? Who would be calling me? Stacey, because Larry had made her unhappy? Too quick for that, so no. Nick, because Brooke was sick? It was still Sunday. My mother?

Well, she might. But it would only be to check on me. She had her own life.

I wondered when I was going to get mine.

CHAPTER 12

When El's mother called on Sunday morning, he steeled himself for hysterics, assuming she'd figured out what they'd done in the attic. She was sunny, though, which made El relax, but not all the way. "What can I do for you, Mom?"

"I wanted to know if you had any lamination machines at the shop. I can't find mine, and I wanted to make the girls some bookmarks out of these great old calendars I found."

I found was Mom-code for *I dug out of someone else's garbage*. El swallowed a nag about how she shouldn't do that and said, "No lamination machines today, I'm afraid."

"Shoot. Well, I'll get myself a backup."

There was only so much nagging one could swallow. "Mom, you don't need another lamination machine. You don't even need *one* lamination machine. I bet you never even took the first one out of its box."

"I did so. I just can't remember where I left it."

He should leave it alone. He knew that. But it was another one of those academic-versus-reality moments. "Tell you what, Mom. You make the bookmarks, bring them to me, and I'll get them laminated."

"Oh, I can't bother you with that."

"It's not a bother. I have a friend with a lamination machine," he lied.

"You do? Can I borrow it?"

"How about when you finish, you bring me the bookmarks, and I'll get them laminated for you?" The odds were good she wouldn't get to that point anyway, but if she did, he'd run them to Staples for her or wherever they did laminating these days.

"That's nice of you to help me, sweetheart. I'll make a bookmark for you too, then."

Never mind that El didn't read books, just newspapers and magazines. "You let me know when you're ready."

The conversation ended shortly after that, but El let himself get wound up over it all the same. He opened the shop like he always did, but within an hour he'd burned through almost half a pack of cigarettes, and the thought of going upstairs to have lunch while he continued to stew over the whole business was more than he could stomach. Closing up the shop, he headed out to pick up something from the deli, thinking the walk would do him good.

When he rounded the corner onto Main Street, he saw Paul standing in the middle of a sidewalk, staring into a shop window with an odd expression on his face.

Normally, El would have boomed out a cheerful, wise-cracking greeting, but something about the way Paul stood gave him pause. He didn't have that lost look he usually had; or rather, he had it, but seemed to be more consumed by it than usual.

It made him come up beside Paul quietly, respectfully, made him smile a crooked smile when Paul saw him. "Hey there, stranger. Any chance I can take you to lunch?"

Paul blinked, as if the concept of lunch was something he'd forgotten. "Oh." He glanced at the clock on the square. "Oh. Lunch. Sure."

"Well, don't let me keep you from staring into shop windows, if you'd rather do that."

Paul winced and rubbed a hand self-consciously on the back of his head. "Sorry. I—had a weird night. Still sorting through it."

El could have kicked himself for sounding so petulant. Placing a hand on Paul's shoulder, El steered him away from the window. "Come to lunch with me, then, and tell me all about it."

Was it El's imagination, or did Paul relax a little? "Okay."

El kept his hand on Paul's shoulder while they walked away. He used the touch to anchor himself as he glanced back to see what it was Paul had been staring at so pensively. It was the photography store's window display with senior pictures on one side.

Wedding pictures were on the other.

Paul didn't tell El about what had upset him, though, because somehow, while they waited in line to place their sandwich orders, they ended up talking about exactly the wrong topic.

El.

"What's it like to own a pawnshop?"

Paul leaned back against the deli's brick wall as he asked this, his red-brown hair a pretty complement to the brick. It did crazy things to El's brain. "It's not really like anything. Just another job."

"How did you get into it, though? Was it something you always wanted to do?"

El laughed. "No."

Paul smiled his own lopsided smile and made *go-on* motions with his hand.

El kept his eye on Paul's hair as he answered, watching light dance off it under the soft track lights. "It was my grandpa's place, his hobby shop once he retired. Nobody wanted it when he died, so I took it over. Bought it from my grandmother, and now it's mine. I live upstairs, work downstairs. Nice and tidy."

Paul studied El with a focus that made him want to fidget. "But did you want to run the pawnshop?"

El considered a moment. Then he did something he rarely ever did when someone asked about the shop. He told the truth.

"Yeah. I did." El rubbed his thumb against his chin a moment, letting his eyes fall down to a set of bricks. "My mom . . . well, you know those TV shows about people who go crazy about collecting things and have houses full of trash? That's my mom. She's been that way since I was little, when my dad left. I know she's sick, and I don't blame her, not really, but it still makes me nuts. I thought maybe if I had a place she could sell things . . ." He let that trail off like it deserved, rolling his eyes and shrugging. "I was a naive twenty-year-old. Now it's a job where I can smoke all day. But yeah. When I took on the shop? I wanted it."

The confession made El feel very exposed, and he wished he could smoke right then and there.

It was their turn to order after that, which saved him for a few minutes. It gave him a chance to redirect his thoughts, too, and he had himself all ready to turn the conversation back onto Paul by the time they sat down.

Paul foiled him by starting it back up on El while they filled their drinks at the self-serve soda machine.

"Do you have any employees, or is it just you?"

"Just me. My brothers have filled in for me on occasion, but mostly if I don't want to be open, I don't keep the shop open."

Paul paused with his cup half-full of Coke and gave El the strangest look of longing. "Really?"

"Really." El elbowed him and reached for a lid. "Why, you looking to buy me out and let me retire early?"

Paul's sad sigh wedged right under the bottom of El's ribs and made them ache in an odd way that only Paul could. "I couldn't afford to buy you out when *I* retire. I'm lucky to make rent."

They settled into a high-backed booth, where the green vinyl complemented Paul's hair rather nicely. "What is it you do, Paul? I'm not sure I ever asked."

There was his adorable blush, except El didn't like the way Paul looked almost ashamed as his cheeks stained. "Nothing, really. I'm a receptionist at a veterinary clinic."

"Are you now? That sounds interesting." El meant it too, but he had the feeling Paul wasn't going to believe him.

"Not as interesting as being the actual vet." Paul shrugged, poking at his sandwich. "That was what I went to school for, but I didn't do well. I never even finished."

"You could go back."

Another shrug. "I guess I had an idea of what being a vet would be like, and the reality is different. There wasn't anything else I wanted to do, and when Nick offered to let my job be full time, it all seemed to fall into place. Now here I am."

"Don't sound so happy about it," El teased him.

That at least earned El a little smile. "It's not that I'm not happy with my job. More like this was never what I planned to do with my life, you know? Like there was a schedule and I got off track and I don't know how to get back on." He made a face. "Sorry. I should have warned you when you asked me to lunch that I was in a funny mood."

El knew the feeling. The same restlessness that had driven him out of the shop seemed to be bulldozing at Paul as well. That realization felt like a spark, as if together their restlessness combined could be something more. Something specific. Something better.

He could hear Denver mocking him already, but he ignored it. "Two questions, the second one dependent on the answer of the first. Number one: what's your shoe size?"

Paul looked wary. And, El thought, perhaps a little intrigued. "Nine. Why?"

El wasn't sure the exact size of what he had in the shop, but it had to be close. "Number two: have you ever been rollerblading?"

Three hours later, when El nearly ran Paul over for the umpteenth time, he gave up trying to climb back to his feet and collapsed, laughing, onto the grass beside the trail. Paul fumbled to the ground beside him, laughing as well. "I assumed when you asked me to rollerblade that *you* knew how."

"Never said that." El shaded his eyes from the afternoon sun. "These have been in the shop for years. I doubt anyone's going to use them, so we might as well."

Paul propped himself up on his elbows and stuck his rollerbladed feet out into the sidewalk. "What do you do when things don't sell?"

"I leave it all as long as I can. If I start running out of room or get tired of looking at something, I take it to Goodwill or throw it out. Generally, I do that less and less as I go on. You start to learn what will sell and what won't and stop taking it."

Except, of course, when he bought kitchen appliances from cute redheads.

Paul stared out across the park toward the amphitheater, where a couple of college kids were horsing around at the edge of the stage. The sun made his hair look like fiery, spun gold and lit up his creamy skin, making El want to touch it. Paul looked wistful, and El wanted to tease him back into happy.

"You make it sound so easy," Paul said.

That made El laugh. "What, pawning people's stuff? It's not rocket science, no."

He shook his head. "Being happy, I mean. Accepting what you have and being happy with it."

That was how he looked to Paul? "I wouldn't say I'm happy."

Now Paul focused on him, his sweet, gullible gaze searching. "You're always laughing and teasing. And you're always so put-together. Nothing upsets you."

El should tease now, he knew that, but he couldn't. "You know what they say about comedians. They laugh so you don't see them cry." Except that was way too far, so he shrugged and turned back to the park. "I'm not unhappy, I guess. Accepting, maybe. Life is what it is. Can't change it, can't quit the game."

But you can avoid playing as much as possible.

Paul didn't seem to like El's answer. "Of course we can change it. We can do better. Find the right thing to say. Plant the right flowers." That made El eyeball him, earning a blush as a reward. "There's a neighborhood contest to make our yards look nicer. I want to win." He scowled into the distance. "Of course, maybe you're right. Maybe I can't win."

"I never said that," El pointed out quickly.

Paul wasn't listening now, though. "I never can. I never have. Not in high school, not in college, and certainly not now." His scowl turned painful. "Larry was mad at Stacey last night, so she came home. To my home. I let her stay."

Why did that confession feel like a bucket of ice water? El tried to sound neutral. "Oh?"

"She slept in bed beside me and nothing happened. Because I didn't want to push her. Because I knew she probably wouldn't want to do anything. Then I woke up and she was talking to him on her phone, everything straightened up. I was a mistake, that's what she told me. I tried so hard to be good and not take advantage, to do what she wanted, and I lost. Again." He'd been ripping up tufts of grass while he spoke, and he tossed a handful out onto the sidewalk in disgust. "Why do I do that? Why do I keep hanging on, trying to be her first choice? I don't even know that I care about her anymore. I just want to be the first choice for someone for once. Just *once*."

El couldn't help but think how, had anyone else appeared in front of him on the sidewalk, even Denver, he would have continued on his solitary way instead of suggesting rollerblading. "I bet you're first choice a lot of times and you don't even know it."

"Well, I want to know it." He looked adorably fierce now. "God, and I want her to see it. I want everyone to see it." He pointed out across the park. "There. *That*. Those two, necking under that tree. Right where everyone can see them. I want *that*."

El's stomach fluttered, and his cock sat up and paid attention. "You want to make out in the park?"

Oh, more adorable blushing. "No. I mean, yes, but not that specifically. I want to be wanted like that. For something. Anything. And I want everyone to see." His flush deepened. "Just once."

The *just once* kept ringing in El's ears as they climbed back to their feet and bladed clumsily back to the pedestrian mall, where they probably weren't supposed to blade but did anyway. They stopped to catch their breath and descended into more juvenile laughter against a recycling bin. El took a moment to enjoy the sight of Paul relaxed and beautiful, not awkward or shy, just Paul, the best thing that had happened to an afternoon. El was aware of strangers watching, getting caught up in his and Paul's mirth, their happiness.

Caught up in it too, El moved before he could check himself, catching Paul's chin and brushing a soft, chaste kiss across his lips.

Paul's startle frightened El back into his own personal space, made him paste on a sideways grin to disguise his panic. Nodding to the audience, trying to make it clear it was all a joke, he quipped, "There. I think everyone saw that."

El was ready for Paul to be offended or upset or grossed out. He had a whole dismissal ready to explain away the impulse as meaningless. Paul only stared at him, though, stunned, slightly confused, and—possibly—touched.

"Thanks," he said at last. A little breathlessly, and that tugged at El's heart like nothing else could have.

He gave Paul a manly pat on the back and a wink. "Come on. First one to smash against the door of the shop has to buy dinner."

CHAPTER 13

T wo days after Stacey had breezed into my life and back out of it again, I stood in my pantry, staring at what was left. I hadn't heard from her. I hadn't bothered trying to call her, either. I grabbed the George Foreman grill and the fondue pot. I wasn't even hard up for cash. It was more about wanting to be rid of the past. I couldn't get over how good it felt to empty my pantry of the leftovers from my relationship with Stacey. Somehow, each new open spot on the shelf felt liberating. Maybe it wasn't quite healing, but it was one less reminder of my inability to be what she'd wanted.

My pulse quickened and fluttered as I maneuvered my box around to open the door to Tucker Pawn during my lunch hour, though I shoved the nerves aside. El had made it clear the kiss wasn't a big deal. A friendly sort of teasing. My reaction was silly, because he hadn't meant anything by it, and we were just friends.

And I wasn't gay, I reminded myself, trying not to be alarmed at how low that truth had fallen on the list of why that kiss shouldn't matter.

El smiled at me, as relaxed and El as ever as he looked up from the counter. "I was wondering when I'd see you again. I need to start paying you less for this stuff so you have to come by more often."

I put the items on the counter, feeling ridiculous at the way my heart kept pounding too hard inside my chest. "I know you said you can only take one item a day, but I really want to get rid of these. The fondue pot can't be worth much anyway, right? I mean, maybe I could give that to you, but you could pay me a bit extra for the other?"

He stared at me. I couldn't tell if he was amused or annoyed. Finally, he smiled. "I'll make an exception," he said. "Since you're my favorite customer."

Pulse, get it together. You're being ridiculous. He's just being friendly. Also, you still are not gay. "Thanks, El."

"But you have to come back after work for the money."

"Why?"

He rubbed the back of his head. "Well, I'll have to fudge a bit on the paperwork, you know—"

"Could you be arrested?" He had said it was some kind of law, and yet it hadn't occurred to me what the cost of breaking that law might be. "I don't want you to do anything that might cause you trouble."

He laughed. Something about it told me I was missing something obvious, like he'd told a joke and I'd missed the punch line. "No trouble. Don't worry about that. Just come back after work."

The afternoon was slow. Two of our patients no-showed. Brooke was sullen and sniffly. I waited for Nick to ask her what was wrong, but he never did. At three o'clock, my mother called me on my cell to give me her flight information. She'd arrive the following Saturday.

Nick ended up sending Brooke home early.

"She won't last much longer," he said to me after she left.

"What do you mean?"

"She and her boyfriend broke up. I bet she'll be moving back home to California."

Then he'd have to hire a new assistant. Hopefully he'd find somebody a bit friendlier.

Right before we closed the office, the door opened, and Velma walked in. She was dressed in tan slacks and a red blouse. Without the tennis skirt and sweater, her resemblance to the cartoon detective was less striking.

"Can I help you?" I asked from my seat behind the counter.

"Hi, Paul. I heard you worked here."

That sounded strangely ominous. I had no idea how to respond.

"I thought I'd stop in and say hi."

"Oh," I said stupidly. "Hi."

"Your yard looks great. The clematis are gorgeous, aren't they?"

"Yeah, they're doing really well. Thanks for the suggestion." I wondered once again if she was one of the Curb Appeal judges. Maybe if I mentioned the contest casually, I'd get a sense of how involved she was. I was trying to figure out how to bring it up when Nick came out of his office. I didn't think I was imagining the way her eyes got a bit bigger when she saw him.

"Oh, hello," Nick said. "I didn't realize we had another appointment scheduled this afternoon." He craned his neck to look over the counter at her feet, obviously looking for the animal he assumed she'd brought with her.

"No, I don't have an appointment." She fidgeted with one of her earrings. "I'm a friend of Paul's."

Nick turned to look at me in surprise, and I tried to erase the look of utter bafflement from my face. She was a friend of mine? When had that happened?

Nick was still staring at me, obviously waiting for an introduction. "This is Dr. Reynolds," I said to her. "Nick, this is…" I came embarrassingly close to calling her Velma, but that wasn't her name.

Too bad I didn't actually *know* her name.

"I'm Lorraine." She held her hand out to Nick.

"Nice to meet you."

She turned back to me. "Hey, Paul. There's this new restaurant that just opened down the block. The Light House. Have you seen it?"

"No." It was pretty stupid to name a restaurant The Light House when we were miles away from any significant body of water.

"I've heard it's really good." She fidgeted with her earring again. "I've been thinking about checking it out."

"Oh." Why was she telling me this? I looked at Nick. He had his head down, ostensibly reading the file he held in his hand, but I could tell he was listening. I could also tell he was highly amused. I had no idea what to say. "You'll have to let us know how it is."

Her smile faded a bit. Nick started coughing.

"Okay," Lorraine said. Her cheeks were as red as her blouse. "Well, it was good seeing you."

"You too."

She left, and I turned back to my computer.

"What's with you?" Nick said. "Are you still that hung up on Stacey?"

"What?" I turned to look up at him, which was a bit of a mistake. He was so confident and good-looking. I always felt intimidated by him. "What do you mean?"

He hooked his thumb toward the door. "That girl. Why didn't you ask her out?"

"I don't know," I said. "Why didn't you?"

"She didn't come to see me."

"She was passing by." Anyway, why would any woman want me to ask her out when Nick was standing right there? Bulging tattooed arms and blue eyes and quirky smile. There was no way I could compete with that. "She wanted to talk about the clematis I put in."

"Clematis," he said, shaking his head in amusement. "Yeah. I bet that's exactly what she had on her mind."

It occurred to me as I was locking up that night that Nick had been hinting Lorraine had been interested in me, as in, *interested*. I blushed at the idea, knowing it was ridiculous. She was a judge for the contest and checking on me. Why would she be interested in me for anything else?

Thank God she wasn't, really, because she wasn't my type. I didn't exactly know what my type was, but it wasn't Velma. Or Daphne either, really. Daphne was too pretty and popular. She'd never go out with me. Velma was too . . . Velma. Did anyone get more sexless than Velma? That only left the boys, and the dog. Obviously not.

Fred was always nice, though. I always thought he'd make a good friend.

I mused over my type all the way home. Someone pulled out of a parking spot just off the square, making me idle in the middle of the street as they pulled away, and I found myself staring across the way at the lights of Tucker Pawn. I thought of El's dark eyes and wicked smile and the way his lips had felt against mine.

The chipmunk screamed, and a car horn brought me back to reality, where the street in front of me was now clear and I was blocking traffic.

I don't have a type, I assured myself, keeping my eyes firmly on the street ahead of me, not allowing my thoughts to drift even for a second to rollerblades, kisses, or the owner of Tucker Pawn.

Of course, before I made it home, I remembered I had to stop at the shop to get my money.

Scolding myself for being absentminded and ridiculous, I drove back. It wasn't like I'd even talk to him much. Probably he'd hand me an envelope without even getting up from his chair. I tried to make the idea seem like a relief instead of a disappointment. Money would be good, I told myself. Maybe I'd treat myself to a big juicy burger for dinner.

El wasn't even smoking when I came in, and he took his time about getting me my money. "So, Paul," he said, after giving me the last of the cash, "how do you feel about ice cream?"

It seemed like a trick question. "Ice cream?"

"Well, it's frozen yogurt, technically. My treat."

What? My heart started beating too fast again. "I haven't even had dinner yet."

He smiled at me. "Life is short, my friend. Let's have dessert first."

How could I say no to that?

The yogurt shop was up the road a couple of blocks, past the unofficial edge of the Light District. We debated driving, but it was too nice a night, so we walked. El gave me a rundown of the things we passed.

"See this bar? It's been here for ages, but they change their name every few years. They keep losing their liquor license for serving to minors."

Next, it was a Starbucks, sitting in one of those strange wedge-shaped buildings on the corner. "This was a brothel once. Upstairs, it was a hotel. I mean, this was way back before the colleges were here. Nobody talks about it. They just say it was a hotel, but my grandma swears it's true. She was a maid there in the sixties, and she says it's still haunted by a whore who was killed in the attic."

Half a block later: "This place here? This used to be the Chamber of Commerce, years and years ago. My dad's granddaddy worked there. He remembers playing in the vault."

A bit further on, it was, "See that horse statue? It looks like wrought iron, but it's brass underneath. Every year, somebody comes down and polishes the dong up all nice and shiny."

A minute later: "This store used to have penny candy. Honest-to-god penny candy. A fucking case of it. I'd take in a dollar, and go home with a bag of Swedish Fish and gum drops."

His enthusiasm for the area was catching, and it made me feel foolish for living here so long and not knowing any of the history. "How long have you lived here?"

"My whole life." He pointed to a bright green door ahead. "Here's the yogurt place. It's kind of new. Hope they don't go out of business."

It was unlike any ice cream store I'd ever been in. They had an entire wall of soft-serve machines, all different flavors, and each one could be swirled with the one next to it. There was an assembly line, almost like a salad bar, but with every type of topping imaginable.

"I like it here," El said. "Other places, seems like I get a lot of ice cream, but then they charge you out the nose for each topping. Here it's by the ounce, so I can get as many toppings as I want."

He was taking full advantage of that, too. The cup in his hand was only half full of chocolate ice cream. He'd topped it with two kinds of chocolate chips, chocolate sprinkles, brownie chunks, and hot fudge. Just looking at it made my throat ache for a glass of water.

"How can you possibly eat that much chocolate at once?" I asked as we left the store.

"Easy. Especially with a coffee chaser. That's our next stop." He leaned over to peer down into my cup. "How many kinds of ice cream you got in there?"

"Three. Coconut Cream, Pistachio Nut, and Raspberry Cheesecake."

He stopped in his tracks, staring at me in apparent horror. "Tell me you're joking."

"No. I put sunflower seeds on top. And Reese's Peanut Butter Cups. And some of that gooey marshmallow topping."

"That's the most disgusting thing I've ever heard."

"It's good."

"It's an abomination, my friend. An insult to frozen yogurt everywhere."

"Don't knock it 'til you try it." I held a spoonful out for him.

He stood for a second, staring at me, maybe trying to decide if I was pulling his leg. Finally, he stepped closer. He touched my wrist with his fingers, as if to make sure I wasn't going to pull away, then leaned forward and let me put the spoon in his mouth.

For some reason I couldn't explain, I expected him to close his eyes, but he didn't. He kept them open, his gaze locked on my face as he took the spoonful of frozen yogurt into his mouth. It made me remember the kiss, the way he'd stood close to me afterward, his gaze full of strange messages that had made me think, for half a second, that he'd meant it to be real.

Right now, I realized I wanted it to be real.

El pulled back from the spoon, but he still held my wrist loosely in his hand. He worked the ice cream in his mouth, watching me carefully as he did for some reason I couldn't fathom. He smiled a bit, and finally, he swallowed.

"See?" I said, my voice shaking. "It's good."

"Not bad at all." His grip became almost a caress, moving down my arm to my elbow.

I blushed, suddenly awkward. And panicked.

"Come on," I said, pulling my arm free. "Let's go get your coffee chaser."

As he and Paul strolled back down the pedestrian mall with their coffees, El acknowledged he had a crush on Strawberry Shortcake. He'd been dancing around it, yes. Obviously that hadn't worked, pretending he wasn't forming a ridiculous attachment. Though he wasn't sure being conscious about it would get him very far, either.

Part of him was obsessed with trying to get Paul to realize he was the object of El's attraction, either so he would blow El off or be offended and horrified, therefore letting El get this nonsense out of his system. But a lot of that desire was also simply wicked curiosity, El wondering if his hand had to be down Paul's pants before he would figure it out. Of course, that made El wonder if he could get his hand down Paul's pants, which was a very dangerous line of thought.

CHAPTER 14

The object of El's affection continued to come in every day the rest of the week with oddball things to sell. Having apparently cleaned out his appliances, he moved on to back massagers and in-home gardening systems and all manner of QVC specials El was never in a lifetime going to unload.

These purchases didn't go unnoticed by Rosa when she came in on Friday afternoon.

"Are you hard up or something? Why are you taking in so much junk?" She lifted the lid of the George Foreman grill and let it fall back down in distaste. "Some little old lady pull on your heartstrings?"

El made a mental note to get rid of Paul's things before someone dangerous wandered into the shop, like Denver or Jase. "Something like that. What's up, sis? If you're in here looking for a babysitter, I sold the last one ten minutes ago."

She gave her patented *yes, you're funny, but not very much* smile. "No. I need you to come by the house tonight for dinner, though."

"You're making me dinner?" El smirked. "Your latest left you already, did he?"

If she'd had a knife in her hand, she'd no doubt have held it up against his throat. As it was, she made do with a glare that cut about as well. "Noah's coming over after he gets off work. I already warned him he might meet my idiot brother who married a pawnshop."

So the boyfriend was still in the picture. *Well, give him a few more minutes.* "He's getting domestic, is he? Hot man doing an evening at home with the mama and her babies? Smart play."

She rolled her eyes. "Noah isn't my boyfriend. He's this guy from work."

This was new. "A guy who's coming over to your house?"

Rosa flicked her finger hard in the center of El's forehead, making him yelp. "*He* is the babysitter. Do you think you could let go of my love life for ten seconds so I could explain about Mom?"

That made El pause. "What about Mom?"

"When she found out I'd given Dante's clothes to Goodwill when he outgrew them, she lost it and started inventorying the house. The kids woke up this morning freaked out because they heard something downstairs. It was Mom going through the cupboards in the garage. I pitched a fit, and she started crying."

El reached for his cigarettes, suddenly tired. "You invited her to dinner too, didn't you. You want me to talk to her."

"Hell, yes, I want you to talk to her. She's not turning my house into Abuela's. I don't give a damn what Uncle Mariano says."

"You think she's going to listen to me? She's going to cry again, and then Uncle Mariano will yell at me, and it'll be the same damn thing as always."

Rosa's jaw was rigid. "It has to stop, El. If Mariano wants to baby her, I'll send all my trash to his house and she can sort through it in *his* garage. I need you there because she upsets the kids, and then I'm trying to yell at her and calm them down at the same time, and it's shit."

She was right. It was nothing but shit. "All right. I'll be there at seven."

"Six. I want her back home before Noah shows up. It's too early for him to see our freaky side." She turned to walk out, shaking her head at the row of appliances as she left. "You *really* fell for that grandma."

She wasn't kidding.

Dinner was spaghetti, meatballs, and baby spinach salad, the latter of which Rosa's kids protested loudly, all but Gabi who happily painted her highchair tray with marinara using the leaves. Patti talked nonstop about pretty much everything under the sun, from who she'd seen at the bank that morning to what Abuela was having for supper, and of course, she told everyone about recent things she had found or bought.

"I found the cutest baby blanket. Absolutely precious, *handmade*. It has a green border and yellow cross-stitched flowers."

Rosa gave El a hard look, and he had to suppress a sigh. *Here we go.*

"Who's having a baby?" he asked.

Patti, unsurprisingly, only shrugged and dug into her spaghetti. "Somebody will have a baby, and then I'll have a present."

"No, you won't, because it'll get buried under your pile of crap," Rosa muttered.

Had she been closer, El would have kicked her under the table. "Mami, we've talked about this."

She was very fixated on her plate now, swirling the noodles in a circle. "It's a blanket. Don't make such a big deal out of it."

"It's a blanket, and a picnic set, and a croquet mallet, and a set of dishes, and that's just the stuff you've told us about. I bet I could go out to your car right now and find all kinds of bags with receipts from today."

Her eyes filled with angry tears. "You shouldn't treat your mother like this."

"And you shouldn't treat your family like this, making us deal with all your trash." Rosa flung her napkin onto the table, ignoring her children's worried glances at each other, except for the baby who was still spinach-painting. "Five-thirty in the morning, Mami. My neighbors saw you going through my stuff."

"Way to let me handle it," El murmured.

Patti was rigid now. "You threw out the baby's things. What else are you going to toss into the trash? My grandbabies' treasures! Someday"— her tears were flowing now—"someday they will thank me for saving their memories."

Rosa started swearing, the kids started whimpering, and the baby, with tomato sauce in her eye, started screaming. Already mentally lighting up a cigarette and drinking a whiskey, El pushed his chair back, herded the kids into their bedroom, and turned on the TV. After cleaning up Gabi, El positioned her in front of *Dora the Explorer* with the others and went back to the argument in the kitchen. Both women were shouting and pointing fingers and, to varying degrees, sobbing, Rosa mostly in fury, Patti largely in hurt. He broke them apart, sending Patti to sit with the kids while he helped Rosa with the dishes, teasing and distracting her until she calmed down.

Patti was still there when Noah showed up, and El liked him on the spot. It was a shame he was the babysitter, not the boyfriend. A little young, but super-sweet and great with the kids, who came running out when they heard his voice, their faces bright and eager. The guy was good: he had a bag of popcorn, three boxes of candy, and a Disney movie in his hand.

"Good to meet you, El," he said when Rosa introduced him, enclosing El's hand in his grip. He was slight, mocha-skinned, and drop-dead gorgeous. Not El's team, though, from the longing looks he cast at Rosa.

El wanted to bang his head on the wall as he realized Rosa had no idea those looks were coming her way.

Noah was gracious to Patti too, giving her the line about seeing where Rosa came by her beauty, which of course El's mom ate up with a spoon. It was all going so well, neither Rosa nor El saw the disaster coming.

"You'll have to come by my house next weekend. We always have a Fourth of July party, and we'd love to have you," Patti said to Noah.

Noah beamed, clearly touched to have been invited. "That'd be great. Usually I get together with my family, but my brother's deployed and my parents have a wedding out of town." He glanced at Rosa. "That okay?"

Rosa said nothing, only stared at El like she wanted him to whip out a gun and put her out of her misery.

"Hey, that sounds great," El said, his mind working overtime, "but the thing is, I've been meaning to talk to you about that, Mom. We should have the party here at Rosa's house. So much more room, and more for the kids to do."

Now Rosa looked like she wanted to kill him. Her house had just enough room to squeeze the kids into it, and that was all.

"Don't be silly. We always have it at Abuela's house," Patti chided.

"Yes, but your projects have gotten very large, haven't they?" It sounded lame, but El couldn't very well say *your hoard*. "With extra people, we'll want room to move around."

It was as if the peace accord hadn't happened. Patti bristled. "One more person isn't too much trouble."

El's head spun as it tried to keep up with his mouth. "Rosa wants to host it, Mami. Besides, I'm bringing someone too."

Rosa and Patti both turned to him, stunned into silence. El was right there with them. What the *fuck* had he said that for? Who the hell was he bringing to Fourth of July?

Paul. You want to bring Paul.

"I don't want to get in the way," Noah objected.

Rosa, thank God, finally came to life. "No—no. It's fine. I want you to come. I was going to ask you myself"—like hell—"but El's right, I wanted to talk about hosting it before I offered. I can't *wait* to have thirty people in my house and backyard. And El can't wait to help me clean up and get ready for it."

Everyone laughed at that, but inside, El was groaning and imagining his very own orphanage again.

As soon as he could escape, El chain-smoked his way down Rosa's street, but once he made it to the Light District, his phone rang. It was Rosa.

"What the fuck, El? I don't want the party at my house!"

"Hey, I was thinking on my feet. Mom had already invited Noah—"

"Then how about I uninvited him later, or something that doesn't upend my life, huh?"

El winced. "I know. Sorry, Rosa. I'll help you clean."

"You'll do *all* the cleaning, you bastard. But first you're going to tell me who you're bringing to the party."

He stopped dead in the middle of the street, panic shafting through him. "Nobody. I was just bullshitting there, trying to sell the reason for moving the party."

"No, that's the bullshit, what you just said to me. When you said you wanted to invite someone, *that* was the truth."

Goddamn Rosa and her ability to see right through him. "It's nobody. Just this guy that's been hanging around the shop. He's a friend."

"A friend you want to fuck. Interesting. What's his name?"

Fuck. "Bob."

"You're lying," Rosa declared, sounding pleased with herself. "Don't worry, I'll get it out of you while you're cleaning." She hung up.

Fuck, fuck, fuck, *fuck.*

Though it hadn't been his original intention, El headed to Lights Out instead of back to the shop. When Denver greeted him at the door, the bouncer's expression changed from welcoming to something heavy and sober.

"Somebody die?" he asked.

"No, but I have the feeling I'm going to wish I had." An idea struck him, and he seized it. "Denver, what are you doing for the Fourth?"

"Working here, what do you think?" He gave El a funny look. "Why?"

"Nothing. I just had this—" He grimaced and shook his head. "Forget it."

Denver grinned at him. "You're looking nervous, buddy. Any chance this nothing has to do with Strawberry? Because if it means I get to watch you with him again, I'll get Jase to find someone else to man the door that night."

Murmuring "Fuck you" under his breath, El nudged past his friend and a gaggle of giggling girls playing tourist, heading straight for Jase and the bar and the alcohol.

CHAPTER 15

I arrived at the office on Monday a few minutes early to unlock, as I usually did. A large cardboard box waited on the sidewalk in front of the door. My first thought was that it was odd for the mailman to have arrived already, but then I heard a scratching from inside.

The cardboard shook, and then I heard something else: a high-pitched, desperate whine.

"Oh no." I got down on my knees, tore open the box, and was immediately attacked by a wriggling ball of black and white fur. "Puppy, who left you here? Are you okay?"

The dog seemed unharmed and eager to be free. "Where'd you come from?" I asked, and the dog lapped its little tongue ineffectually in the direction of my face.

There was a note inside the box.

> This is MoJo. She's a good dog, but I have to go home, and I can't take her with me.
>
> Please take care of her.

"MoJo?" I said to the dog, and her wriggling went into overdrive. She was a small dog, and shaggy. My guess was that she was a Lhasa Apso mix, not more than two years old. She had ears as expressive as Yoda's and about the same shape. "Poor MoJo. How long have you been here? I can't believe your owner left you! What a bad, mean owner." I was talking like an idiot to her, but she clearly liked it. Her little tail whipped back and forth so fast it dragged the bulk of her backside along with it. "Are you hungry? Want something to eat?"

By the time Nick arrived, MoJo was happily snarfing down a can of dog food like she hadn't eaten in days.

"Where'd he come from?" Nick asked.

"She," I corrected. I showed him the note. "Somebody left her on the step."

He shook his head. "I'll never get why people do that. There's a shelter two miles away."

"They probably worry they won't get adopted, but think if they bring them here, you'll take care of them."

"Looks like this one's on you," he said.

"What do you mean?"

"I'm maxed out on dogs. I have three, which is already one more than my lease allows, and they're all big. They'd think that little thing was nothing but an interactive squeaky toy."

"I can't have dogs at my house," I said.

"Too bad." Nick shrugged. "Well, she can hang out here today. I'll drop her at the shelter on my way home."

The shelter. Yes. That was logical. That was the right thing to do. A good dog like her would be adopted in no time.

Probably.

And if not . . .

Well, maybe it was a no-kill shelter? Maybe I should call and ask?

MoJo finished her breakfast and spent half the morning attacking my shoelaces, and most of the afternoon napping at my feet, and meanwhile I spent every free moment picturing her locked in a cage. Not being adopted. Being put to sleep. All because her owner hadn't understood the obligation involved in owning a dog.

All because I couldn't have pets.

By the time we closed for the day, I knew there was no way in hell I was letting Nick take her to the shelter. The problem was, I really couldn't take her home. There was no way in hell I could afford to pay the $5,000 damage clause listed in my lease if caught with a pet. Granted, I might be able to get through the first night without the landlord knowing, but what would I do with MoJo the next day? Or the day after that? I couldn't risk leaving her alone in the house. Nick was a nice guy, but I couldn't ask to bring her to work every day.

Who did I know that could take her? Not Stacey. Not Nick. Not Brooke, who had been sullen all day at work again, sneering at poor MoJo. I didn't have any other friends. The only other person I knew was Emanuel. And I barely even knew him.

Still, barely was better than not at all.

It was absurd, but it was the best idea I had. I took one of Nick's extra leashes and led MoJo down the street to the pawnshop. El was in his usual spot, feet on the counter while he read a newspaper. No cigarette, but it was probably only a matter of time. He looked up when I came in, and I thought maybe he even looked happy to see me.

"Hey, Paul. Here for another beer?"

"No. I have a question for you." I was blushing, unsure what to say. *Can you adopt this dog?* suddenly seemed a bit too forward. He solved my dilemma by standing up and looking down at MoJo in amusement.

"What the hell is that?"

I frowned. "It's a dog. What's it look like?"

He laughed. "That, my friend, is what happens when a gremlin fucks an Ewok."

"Be nice." I reached down to scoop MoJo up off the floor. She wiggled in my hands, her tail wagging and her tongue flapping gleefully toward my face. I put her down on the glass countertop, facing Emanuel. "Look at that face. How can you not love it?"

Emanuel cocked his head sideways at MoJo, as if he really were trying to decide if he could love her or not. MoJo panted happily at him, her tail swishing back and forth on the countertop.

"I hate to break it to you, but you can't pawn a live animal."

"I'm not trying to pawn her. I was wondering if . . ."

"If what?"

I took a deep breath and said in a rush, "If maybe you'd keep her?"

"Like pet-sitting? For how long?"

"Well, uh, forever, I guess. Owning a dog is a full-time responsibility, and—"

El's eyebrows rose into his hairline. "Owning? Who said anything about me owning her?"

"Well, that's what I'm asking. She needs a home."

He crossed his arms over his chest and smiled challengingly at me. "What's wrong with yours?"

"I can't have dogs."

"And why me?"

"You're the only person I know."

He'd looked flummoxed before, but now he seemed flustered. "What am I supposed to do with her?"

MoJo was still on the counter, looking back and forth between us as we talked, her tongue lolling. "I don't want to take her to the shelter. She's a good dog, and I'd worry every single day about whether or not she'd been adopted."

El rubbed the back of his head, staring at MoJo in exasperation. "Not sure I'm allowed to have dogs in here."

"I thought the cops didn't care about your personal vices?"

For half a second he stared at me, as if weighing my words, and then he laughed, his eyes suddenly bright. He rubbed the back of his head again. "Fair enough." He looked down at MoJo, who was responding to the happy tones of our voices, wagging her tail faster than ever, panting at him. "You want to be a pawnshop dog?"

She flapped her tongue excitedly in his direction.

"Huh," Emanuel said. "I had it wrong."

"What?"

He took a red felt-tip marker out of the jar next to the register before turning his back on me, taking something off the shelf behind him, and leaning over it with the marker. A second later, he turned back around and put the item on the counter next to MoJo. It was a soccer ball, white and black, only now it sported a little red half-moon in one of the white spots. He turned MoJo around so she was facing me.

Black and white. The tip of her tongue hung from her mouth, a little half-moon of pink.

Emanuel held his hand over them and pointed back and forth between them. "See the resemblance?"

I laughed. "Does that mean you'll take her?"

"I guess." He leaned down to look at MoJo, staying out of reach of her tongue. "No peeing in the store. No chewing the skis or the golf clubs. No biting the customers, unless I give you the signal. Got it?"

MoJo's wriggling turned into full-blown convulsions of doggy glee.

"I think she's got it," Emanuel said, standing up straight again to face me.

"Thanks, El. Really. I'll pay for her food if you want—"

"Forget it. What's she weigh? Two pounds? She obviously doesn't eat much."

I looked at MoJo, still sitting on the counter next to the defaced ball. They were about the same size. The resemblance really was uncanny. "Dogs aren't for kicking."

He laughed. "Don't worry. I never even played soccer."

I spent the next morning wondering how MoJo was doing. Brooke had called in sick again, and we were too busy for me to take a lunch break. Finally, at around three, I looked up the number for Tucker Pawn and called.

"Tucker Pawn," El said, curt and to the point.

"El, it's Paul."

"Hey there." I could tell he was smiling. "I thought you'd be by at lunch to check on this dog."

"I couldn't get away. How's she doing?"

"Well . . ." I could picture him rubbing the short hair on the back of his head. "I don't know, man. She doesn't seem good, you know."

"Oh no! What's wrong? Is she depressed?"

"Maybe—"

"Her owner did leave her. Is she eating?"

"She eats, yeah, but—"

"Is she vomiting?"

"No, but—"

"But she's not doing well? That's what you said, right?"

"Well, I don't know much about dogs. I think you better come check on her. I think you'd feel better seeing her for yourself."

"I will," I promised. "I'll come by after work."

Of course that meant another two hours of worrying. Being abandoned was hard on an animal. Some people claimed dogs didn't have feelings like people, but I knew that wasn't true. I'd seen dogs who were depressed or lonely. I hoped that wasn't the case with MoJo.

Five o'clock finally came. I took a handful of dog treats out of our cookie jar before locking the door and heading to the pawnshop. Maybe they'd help cheer her up.

I walked in the door, and my ankles were immediately under siege. MoJo ran around my feet, trying to climb up my leg any time I held still.

"Hey, girl," I said, bending to feed her a treat. "How are you doing? Are you sad?"

She didn't look sad, though. She ran gleefully around my feet, then sat up on her haunches, begging for another treat.

I looked up at El, who was standing behind the counter, watching us. "She looks fine," I said.

"Does she?"

"She does to me. What had you worried?"

"Well, I don't know that I was worried . . ."

"You said she wasn't doing well, but she looks perfectly happy."

"Well, yeah," he said. "But that's part of the problem, see? She doesn't do what she's told. Watch. MoJo, act sad."

MoJo glanced over at him, panting happily.

"MoJo, be sad."

MoJo sat down to look up at me expectantly, still waiting for another treat. Her tail thumped against the floor.

"MoJo, bite Paul."

MoJo sat up on her haunches and whimpered at me pathetically. A string of doggy drool hung from her jaw.

"MoJo! I told you to look vicious."

MoJo gave up begging. She turned and ran to El. There was a strange pile of electronic equipment on the floor next to the counter. I wondered what it was for until MoJo clambered up it to sit on the countertop in front of El.

"You built her a staircase?"

"No," El said, scratching MoJo's ears. "I needed a place to store that stuff."

I couldn't help but laugh. It was so obvious the things had been put there specifically for her to climb up. "You're lying."

He shrugged. "Maybe." He looked at the pile of old stereo components. "God help me if anybody decides to buy that 1972 cassette player from the bottom of the pile."

I gave MoJo the last of the treats from my pocket. She gobbled them up, then panted at me, hoping for more.

"She looks fine," I said.

"Well, like I said, I don't know much about dogs. It seemed like a good idea for you to come down and make sure."

It made me smile. I'd done the right thing in asking him to adopt her. "Thanks for taking her. I'm so glad she's happy."

"I'm glad *you're* happy."

His words made me blush for a reason I couldn't quite define, but he didn't give me a chance to respond.

"Listen, I have to help my sister with something tonight, but are you free tomorrow? Maybe we could have dinner."

Was he asking me out? Like a date? The panic I'd carefully packed away since the ice cream incident came rushing back.

He cleared his throat nervously. "For MoJo," he said. "I think she'd like to see you."

I found myself smiling. "You bet," I said. "For MoJo."

CHAPTER 16

"Y ou got a dog." Denver shook his head in disbelief. "And you're carrying it in a baby sling. Who are you, and what have you done with El?"

El gave Denver the finger and started to fish MoJo out of the carrier, pausing to hand Denver the leash. "Here, hold this. I need to put her down so I can have a cigarette."

"Seems like it'd be easier with her all tucked cozy like that."

"Yes, but I don't want to give her that close a dose of secondhand smoke."

Denver's eyes went wide, and he held up his hands as he backed away. "Now you're freaking me out."

Yanking the leash out of Denver's hand, El clipped the lead to MoJo's collar and encouraged her to explore the outside of Tucker Laund-O-Rama while he slipped the other end over his wrist and fiddled with his cigarette. "It's a favor for a friend," he murmured after he'd taken a long draw.

Denver relaxed significantly. "Hey, you never answered me about the Fourth. Jase says I could have it off if I want, but I had to give a full report."

El waved him away. "Forget it. Dumb idea."

Denver grunted and raised his eyebrows, but didn't press the issue. "So we forget the Fourth. Tell me about the dog. You're babysitting. Oh, this must be for Strawberry."

El averted his eyes. "No, I adopted the dog. But as a favor. Look, you can go in and get started. I won't be long."

"The hell you get off that easy. What the fucking fuck, El? You adopted a dog for this kid?"

"Paul's not a kid." El inhaled half the cigarette in one furious draw, at least metaphorically. "But yeah. I took in MoJo because Paul asked."

All signs of teasing died in Denver's face. "Shit. You're serious about him. Like, serious, serious. Holy fuck."

"Nothing is happening." El sighed and leaned back against the wall, nudging MoJo away from the smoke stream as she came back to explore his feet. "He has no idea. I fucking kissed him and he's still clueless. It's cute, but it's also clear he isn't interested. At all. On any level of any kind."

"Except to ask you to adopt a dog, which you gladly do. Shit. And he didn't even figure *that* out?" Denver looked wary now. "Is he . . . you know, mentally challenged?"

"Fuck off."

"I wasn't joking, El. I mean, I'm not going to judge. I'm trying to figure this out. Nothing about this is like you at all."

El didn't answer, because it was true. He finished his cigarette and whistled to MoJo, who trotted happily after him inside.

"Nothing's going to happen," El said to Denver as they settled on their plastic benches, watching MoJo try to bite at some itchy spot on her back as their clothes entered the first spin cycle. "He isn't interested. I'm just a friend to him. I wondered for a minute, but I don't even think he's gay. Or if he is, he's not interested in acting on it."

Denver was quiet so long El thought he'd fallen asleep or something. When he glanced over, however, Denver had this weird look on his face, something between disgust and disappointment. "What?" El complained. "Why are you looking like that? What did I do?"

Denver took so long to answer, El wasn't sure he would. "You know, you're probably my best friend, if I'm even capable of having such a thing, which is the only reason I'm saying this at all. Otherwise I'd let you go off and be an idiot." He held up a meaty hand when El tried to protest. "You carry on about your sister picking up guys at bars and me taking home vapid twinks from Lights Out, saying we're deliberately setting ourselves up for a fall to keep ourselves in a negative relationship pattern or however you spin that bullshit. Well, pot, this mooning over someone who isn't gay or won't act on it and doesn't realize you're into him, this guy you're fucking adopting puppies for? It ain't any different than what we kettles are doing."

El stared at MoJo for almost a full minute before he could say anything, and even then all he could manage was, "Watch the dog. I'm going out for another cigarette."

The thing was, El knew Denver was right. He *was* doing exactly what drove him crazy in other people. Plus he was dragging it out by always making sure Paul had an out: that when they met they were having dinner for MoJo, not each other, that El was just teasing when he kissed him, that nothing El did meant anything at all because they were just friends, Paul was straight, and El didn't date. Except El wanted to be more than friends, wanted desperately for Paul to be gay, and despite all his protestations, yes, he wanted to date. He wanted to bring him to the family party and show everyone his adorable new boyfriend.

Which meant first he'd have to ask Paul to be his boyfriend. Which meant he'd have to give up his vow to never date anyone.

El thought about his mental one-eighty a lot when he went over to Rosa's to help her get ready to host the Fourth party and found Noah there yet again. It turned out he'd asked to be allowed to help, and he'd kept asking until Rosa had caved. Right now he was setting up a second grill in the backyard, next to the one El had already loaned her from the shop. Noah said it was his, except he was unpacking it brand-new from a box. And it was a damn nice grill.

Rosa still didn't notice how hard Noah had tried to impress her, just as she hadn't noticed the long, lingering looks he'd been giving her. She was too busy needling El about his unnamed date and complaining about what a disaster the last boyfriend had been. She regaled him with stories, too, about this new guy she'd spotted when she'd met some of the girls for drinks at the martini bar. It seemed the cluelessness-in-love thing was going around.

What sent El over the edge, though, was when he ducked out of the shop to grab some lunch on the day of his dinner date with Paul, and saw Paul seated at an outdoor café.

Smiling. Laughing.

At his lunch date.

A girl.

El ducked behind a bush and watched them for half an hour, keeping MoJo quiet with biscuits he'd started storing in his pockets. El didn't go up and say hello to Paul, no matter how MoJo whined and tugged on her lead, because he wasn't sure he could do it without dumping coffee into the lap of that dizzy bitch with nerd glasses and a bowl cut. The dizzy bitch who smiled and flirted with Paul, who kept touching his arm, who Paul didn't withdraw from, who seemed to make Paul flustered and nervous.

The dizzy bitch Paul wasn't oblivious to.

El stayed there so long he ended up having to whip together peanut butter and graham crackers in his own kitchen so he could get back to the store in time for an appointment with a guy who wanted to pawn a vintage jukebox. He smoked his way through a whole pack that afternoon, until he felt like the big, messy crap MoJo made after eating the pile of biscuits he'd fed her while they spied on Paul. He made a bad deal on the jukebox because he was too preoccupied with the way the nerd glasses and bowl cut had undressed Paul with her eyes.

Then he stood in the shower until MoJo whined at the door and the water ran cold, his head against the wall, acknowledging he didn't just have a crush on Paul. He was head-over-idiot-heels.

He was going to have to do something about it.

CHAPTER 17

I got home from work late because Brooke had called in sick again and Lorraine had found me on my lunch break and held me captive, talking about Bill and his yard and how she'd suggested all these things to help him make it better. I'd assumed it was to make me jealous over her defection to him for the contest, which completely worked.

Brooke being out meant I got to help Nick with the animals again, but it also meant I ended up covered in hair, slobber, and vomit by the end of the day. Even though I was cutting it close, I decided to run home and change before meeting Emanuel for our date.

If that's what it was.

What if it *was* a date?

The idea made my heart do strange, acrobatic things inside my chest, dredging up feelings long, long since packed away in the deep recesses of my mind. I remembered my fumbling encounters back in high school with a neighbor boy. They had been fun. Thrilling, even. The bright, heart-racing excitement of discovering something new. Of course, *everything* had been new back then. I was older now. No longer a virgin.

How much different would it be with a man? And especially with somebody as confident as El?

The panic returned in force, the chipmunk finally finding its feet in this argument. No, no, I didn't want to be with a man. I'd turned away from that a long time ago. It was a good thing, too, because being with a man was the wrong track to take in life. With Stacey, I would have had all the things I was supposed to have. A house. A family. A place in the normal world doing normal things like winning Curb Appeal contests. The *right* things. The way it was supposed to be.

A new voice tried to reach me, asking why I had to be with a woman to have those things, but the chipmunk, renewed of purpose, started chirping in earnest, and I moved my thoughts to other things in self-defense.

The truth was, I had other things to occupy my mind. My mother was planning to come for the Fourth of July. She would arrive in four days and be with me for five. Nick had offered to give me the week off, but although I felt I should take the time to spend with my mother, the truth was, I couldn't afford to miss out on a week's worth of pay. I wasn't sure how she'd keep herself occupied. I also didn't know that much about Tucker Springs, like the best places to eat. Maybe I could take her to the Light House.

I was surprised when I pulled up in front of my house to find Stacey's car in the driveway. I hadn't talked to her since the night she'd come to my house crying. I wasn't sure how I felt about seeing her again now. The question was, which Stacey would I find? The one who missed me, or the one who'd told me not to call again?

She apparently still had a key and had let herself in, because the front door was unlocked. "Hello?" I called as I walked in.

"Paul?" she called back from the direction of the kitchen. I could tell by her voice that she was unhappy about something. "Where's the panini press?"

I groaned. I didn't want to see the look on her face when I told her I'd sold everything. I went into the bedroom instead and started changing my clothes.

"Paul?" she said again. She was getting closer.

Maybe I could escape out the window.

"Paul?" she said, this time from the door of the bedroom. "Answer me. Where's my panini press?"

"*Your* panini press?" I said as I tossed my soiled shirt into the hamper. "If it's *yours*, then it must be at *your* house." I yanked a clean shirt off the hanger in the closet. "Or maybe it's at Larry's."

"Don't be a smartass, Paul. I came by to pick it up, and it's gone."

"I sold it."

"You *what*?"

"You heard me." I started to unbutton my pants, but stopped to glare at her. "Do you mind? I'm trying to change."

She rolled her eyes. "Give me a break. As if I've never seen you without your pants."

Of course that was true, but it still annoyed me to have her standing there, glaring at me with her arms crossed. I took my pants and went in the bathroom, slamming the door shut behind me.

"And what about all the other stuff?" she asked from the other side of the door. "The cappuccino maker and the bread machine?"

"I sold those too."

"You had no right to do that, Paul. Those were my things!"

"Your things?" I was done changing clothes, and I opened the door to face her. "Your things? They've been here for months! You left them here, Stacey. Just like you left me."

This caught her off guard, but only for a second. "Still—"

"You left me here in this shitty fucking house to make a rent payment that my paycheck barely covers. You moved right in with Larry. God knows how long you'd been fucking him before you finally left. And now you show up at *my* house and let yourself in with a key you should have left behind, and you say I had 'no right' to sell *your* fucking panini press? The panini press I bought for you for our anniversary?"

She took a step backward, her mouth a small round O of surprise. In all of our years together, I'd never been as angry at her as I was at this moment. I'm not sure I'd ever been this angry in my life.

"I'm leaving now," I told her. "And so are you. And I suggest you leave your key behind, because the next time I come home and find you here without my permission, I'm calling the cops."

"Oh, for fuck's sake, Paul. How dare you?"

"If there's anything else you want," I said, "anything you actually think you have a right to, you'd better take it now. Otherwise, get the fuck out."

To my surprise, she didn't argue. She took one thing from the pantry: the turkey fryer. I was pretty sure it was more an attempt to annoy me than because she wanted it.

She left her key on the kitchen table.

I should have felt victorious, but I didn't. I was mad, but the chipmunk worried its hands, urging me to run after her and apologize. I was almost ready to do that, but what I saw when I finally opened my front door made things worse. Bill was in his yard. He'd put up a strange little decorative hook. It held a bright flag that said *Happy Fourth of July*. He was standing at the curb, talking to Velma.

Except her name was Lorraine.

"It's cute as can be," I heard her say, though she looked right at me, cheeks flushed with her triumph as she preened at her new contest favorite. "If you put in a few more flowers by the porch, and maybe a birdbath—"

"That's a great idea," he said.

She kept walking, and Bill watched her go, bouncing a little on his feet. He looked over at me. He was practically gloating.

Goddamn Bill and his cute little flag and the motherfucking Curb Appeal contest. I had no doubt he'd have a birdbath by Sunday. And what did I have?

I looked out at my lawn, which suddenly seemed far less inviting than it had.

All I had was the fucking *Detroit Daisy* and a goddamned one-legged chicken.

"I told you to take whatever you thought was yours," I mumbled.

It took a significant amount of effort to wrangle the chicken into the backseat of my old Volvo, its head or top or whatever the apex of it was sticking out of the rear window like a demented dog. Bill watched me from his lawn, frowning slightly. I didn't really know what I thought I was doing with the damn thing. I only knew I wanted it gone.

That seemed like enough, right up until I pushed my way through the door of El's shop with the thing propped precariously on my shoulder. It was damn heavy.

"What the fuck is that?" El asked as I set it down. MoJo came running over to investigate. I half hoped she'd pee on it.

"It's art," I said.

"Only in Hacktown." He raised his eyebrows and scratched the back of his head, and I noticed his hair was damp, like he'd taken a shower. "I know I adopted this damn dog, but I'm not sure I can take that monstrosity."

"I don't care what you do with it," I said. "I just don't want to have to see it every day."

He pursed his lips, as if thinking it over. "Well, I'll figure something out." He smiled at me. "You ready to go?"

"Sure."

He took a bright piece of fabric that looked almost like a giant purse from a hook behind him. He looped it over his head. "What is that?" I asked.

"It's a baby sling. Couple of years ago, I thought I'd start a maternity department. Turns out nobody wants to buy baby stuff from a pawnshop. I still had this lying around."

He whistled at MoJo. She ran to him, clambering expertly up the staircase of stereo equipment to the countertop. El held the sling open, and she climbed inside. After a bit of squirming and turning, she finally settled down against him. Only her head stuck out of the sling. She was panting happily up at him.

"You look ridiculous," I said.

"Says the man with the one-legged chicken."

He had a point.

I waited for him to lock the door, then followed him down the street. "What's got you all riled up?" he asked.

"Is it that obvious?"

He shrugged.

"Stacey came by."

"Ah," he sighed. "Enough said."

We were silent the rest of the way. He finally led me into a small, dark bar. "The food here's better than you might think," he said. "But it's better out back, on the patio."

"No dogs allowed," the bartender yelled as El led me past.

"Good to know," El said. But he didn't stop, and the bartender waved him on. I had the feeling he hadn't expected El to pay any attention.

The patio was surrounded by a wrought iron fence. El let MoJo out of her sling. There were four tables, one of which was occupied by two women who immediately went gaga over the dog.

"The bartender said no dogs," I worried.

"I know the owner," El said. "He won't mind."

I hadn't realized how hungry I was until I started looking over the menu. Everything sounded good.

"Will you share a pizza with me?" I asked El.

His eyes danced and he winked at me. "I'll do anything you like."

I blushed and ducked my head. The waitress arrived, saving me from my embarrassment. I ordered the pizza and El ordered drinks—a Coke for himself, but a rum and Coke for me.

"Keep them coming," he said to the waitress. "My friend's had a bad day."

For better or worse, the waitress obliged.

CHAPTER 18

By the time El and Paul finished the pizza, Paul had also polished off three rum and Cokes. When asked if he wanted to go home or to Lights Out, he grinned drunkenly and slurred something about dancing. It was the first time in El's life that dancing sounded like the best idea ever.

El went to the other end of the patio, called Rosa, and begged and pleaded with her to take MoJo until the morning. After a quick stop by her house, where he admitted that yes, he was on a date, El escorted Paul past the line to the front door of the bar. Ignoring Denver's pointed look, he tightened his grip on Paul's hand and led him to the dance floor.

Intellectually and probably morally, El knew he should switch Paul to water, but it hadn't escaped his notice that the more alcohol he let Paul take in, the more Paul leaned on him and the heavier Paul's hands rested on El's hips while they danced. Plus, Drunk Paul laughed. A lot. Beautifully.

"This is so much fun," Paul said for the tenth time as they sank against the bar near the stairs leading to Jase's office. "I haven't been dancing in . . ." He looked confused for a moment, then laughed. "I don't know. I don't think I've ever danced like this."

"That's because you haven't had the right partner." El made the comment lighthearted, but his solar plexus felt like it was trying to explode. Insanity burst through that dam anyway, making him add, "Of course, you haven't really been dancing at Lights Out until you've made out on the dance floor."

Though El was ready for Paul to shut down at that, or make a disgusted face, or miss his point entirely as usual, Paul's response was an almost feral grin. "You've kissed me before. As a joke, I know. But you kissed me."

It hadn't been a joke. "Oh?"

Paul's grin widened and he put his hand on El's thigh, sending the blood from El's head straight to his cock. "Did you know you weren't the first guy who kissed me?"

Suddenly El didn't have knees. "Oh?"

"The neighbor boy. In high school." Paul's hand massaged El's thigh. "Dean. We kissed and rubbed against each other until we came in our underwear."

"Jesus." El started to shake. A little more of this talk and young Paul and Dean wouldn't be the only ones who'd creamed their pants.

Paul's hand stilled as he tilted his head to the side and sobered. "El, are you gay?"

El would have laughed if he'd had enough air left in his lungs to do it. "Yeah."

Paul bit his lip, looking guilty. El wanted to pull that lip out and bite it himself. While jacking Paul's cock. "So would you mind?"

Mind jacking his cock? Biting his lip? Hell no. "Huh?"

Paul's blush about did El in. "Kissing me. On the dance floor."

El was so far down the rabbit hole, the world was upside-down. He never wanted it to go right-side-up again. "Sure."

Pulse pounding in time to the music, El led Paul back out to the dance floor, his cocky smile the only marker of nerves as he pulled Paul in tight against his body. El wanted to put his hand down the back of Paul's jeans, but he settled for taking firm hold of his ass and pulling him up against his own erection.

Oh, God, Paul was hard. So hard El could feel his cock thick and heavy as it pressed against his own through their clothes.

Swallowing the glib excuse he'd prepared, the pathetic out so he could pretend he didn't want to do this, El admitted, at least to himself, that kissing Paul in this moment meant everything in the world to him. He was hard. Paul was hard. They both wanted it.

So El kissed him.

Really kissed him, stealing deep inside with his tongue, every nerve ending in his body going wild as he took his first slick, rum-and-Coke taste of Paul. When Paul went slack, El dove in again, deeper this time, mating with Paul's tongue like his life depended on it. Drawing back, he nipped hard enough on Paul's bottom lip to make him squeak, then went in for a third time.

They kissed on the dance floor, and everything was right. El kept his hands on Paul's ass and kissed him until they both lost their knees. El's hands slid up underneath Paul's T-shirt, stuttering against his sweaty skin until he started kneading at the slight muscles of Paul's back. Eventually, one palm did make it under Paul's waistband, seeking the soft, sweet flesh of his now-quivering backside, while the fingers of El's other hand found their way, still under Paul's shirt, to a nipple. All the while, he kissed Paul without stopping, sucked on his lips, his tongue, traced the outline of his teeth. Swallowed his gasps. Held up his shuddering body while he came unglued and El devoured him like a man who hadn't kissed anyone like this in years.

Which was exactly what El was.

It wasn't until someone bumped into them that El realized they'd stopped dancing entirely, that he'd started undoing Paul's pants and was ready to sink to the floor so he could take Paul in his mouth. Not that something like this was completely out of line at Lights Out.

But all of this absolutely was for Paul—especially drunk off his ass.

Paul blinked out of his haze, and guilt swamped El as he took in his swollen lips and bloodshot eyes. "Why—why did you stop?"

Not because he wanted to, that's for damn sure. "I should get you home."

The way Paul's face closed up, all that easiness and happiness and something that sure looked like lust evaporating, made El's heart clench. "I don't want to go home."

Then how about you come to my place? "Paul, you've had a lot to drink."

"So what? Everyone here has."

He had a point. El wanted to give into it, but he didn't let himself. "I need to get you home." *I don't want you to regret this in the morning.*

I don't want you to never want to see me again in the morning.

It was the right thing to do. El knew it was. But no amount of knowing that could have prepared him for the look of rejection, of disappointment, of *humiliation* on Paul's face as he turned away from El and disappeared into the crowd.

CHAPTER 19

W alking away from El on the dance floor was a mistake, not because I wanted to stand there and be told I was a baby and had to go home, but because he was right; I was drunk, incredibly so, and within thirty seconds I was lost, disoriented, and a little scared.

However, when he grabbed my arm and hauled me off the dance floor, I got mad again.

I didn't know why I was mad, but I was. Furious, actually, and embarrassed, but mostly just mad. Confused too, I guess, but that mostly made me angry too. Something had happened. I wasn't sure what, but something big had happened, and then I'd lost it, and now I felt like half a cantaloupe someone had hollowed out.

And El wanted to take me home and leave me there because I was drunk.

Maybe it was because of the kiss on the dance floor, I realized, as he poured me into his car and headed toward my house. I kept my eyes on the blurry streetlights so I wouldn't have to see the truth of that in his face, if it was the case. Which it probably was. I'd kissed too hard. I'd asked for it and he was disgusted.

Except he hadn't seemed disgusted. Except for at the end when he'd declared I had to go home.

Except I'm not gay! The thought flared up like a dud firecracker and died an ignoble death.

How could I ask a gay man to make out with me on the dance floor of a gay bar and *not* be gay?

I was so confused. And hollow. And empty.

And sad.

I was all ready for El to drop me off at my curb, but he put his car in park, killed the engine, and came around to my door before I could figure out how to open it. He put an arm around me, too, helping me up the walk.

It made me sadder still.

"What the hell is that?" he asked, nodding at *Detroit Daisy*.

"Art." I scowled at it. "It's too heavy, or I'd have brought it to your shop."

"Thank God." He squeezed my elbow. "Come on, honey. Let's get you inside."

He came into the house with me, still hovering like he was my mother, which made me angry again. "I have to go to the bathroom," I said, pulling free and heading for it without waiting to hear what he said. I assumed he would be gone when I came out. I did have to go to the bathroom, but when I was done I splashed water on my face, and then, figuring I was going to bed now, I brushed my teeth too. I sat down on the lid of the toilet for several minutes when I was done, wallowing in my confusion and misery and giving El adequate time to get out.

When I came out of the bathroom, El's car was still at the curb, but El wasn't in the kitchen or the living room. I found him in my bedroom, standing beside my bed, holding up Stacey's ring with an odd expression on his face.

"Why haven't you ever brought this in? I could give you a lot more for it than for all those kitchen gadgets."

I shrugged, staring at the ring in his long dark fingers. It had never occurred to me to try to sell it. Somehow, I'd assumed it would always be here waiting for her.

He let the ring fall into his palm and hefted it, as if testing its weight. He looked up at me. His eyes were guarded. "You still love her?"

"I don't know. I thought I did, but . . ." I was trying to kick my shoes off, which was significantly more difficult than normal. I let my words die away as I concentrated on first one, then the other.

"But what?" he prompted.

"Maybe it's been a long time since I loved her." I had to hold onto the footboard while I pulled off my socks. "I loved the life we were supposed to live."

"What's that mean?"

I couldn't answer. I couldn't tell him of the plans Stacey and I had made, me with a veterinary practice, her selling her art. Buying a house. Having kids. Seeing my mother's joy when she became a grandmother. Tennis with friends in the morning and cocktails in the afternoon. Mr. and Mrs. Hannon. A cookie-cutter life. That's what Stacey had always wanted.

"Paul?"

It was too much. The hollowness threatened to swallow me, and I blinked hard. "Forget I said it."

He didn't answer, and I didn't dare look at him. I wouldn't have been able to read his expression anyway. I pulled my shirt off and dropped it on the floor, then my pants. I wanted to go to bed and have this day be over. I didn't want to think about it anymore.

Stacey had always been the one who made the bed. It hadn't been intact since she'd left. The covers were in a pile at the foot of the bed. Sorting them out now seemed like entirely too much work, so I lay down without them in my briefs and tried not to think about the ring in El's hand, or what it had once represented.

"I take it you're going to bed."

"Yes." Maybe when I woke up, I wouldn't be such a failure.

He hesitated for a long time, then said, "Aren't you afraid I'm going to hit on you?"

I closed my eyes and told myself the sting behind them was only a result of the alcohol. It had nothing to do with being rejected after making a fool of myself in public, in front of El. Of being rejected by El. By everyone in my goddamned life. "I can't imagine you're that desperate."

He didn't answer, but a second later, I felt the bed shift.

I opened my eyes to find him looming above me, straddling my legs, supporting himself above me on his left arm so he could look into my eyes. What I saw there made my breath catch in my throat.

"Is that what you think? That I'd have to be desperate to want you?"

His gaze was so intense, and I swore I could feel heat coming off his body. The chipmunk chattered desperately, but the alcohol made it seem very far away. A new voice, however, began to purr.

"I fail at everything," I said, trying to put us back on more familiar ground.

He didn't even blink. "No, you don't."

"I'm always second. I'm not the vet; I'm the vet's secretary. I'm Stacey's second choice. I'm even in second place in the damn Curb Appeal contest."

He smiled. The gentle warmth in his eyes eased the ache in my chest, and if the chipmunk was still going, I couldn't hear him anymore. "The only thing wrong with you is that you're so sure there's something wrong with you."

I didn't answer. I could only stare at him—his dark skin and his soft, full lips. I wondered if I dared touch him. Thinking about it made the pit of my belly ache in a gloriously sensual way. He still had his clothes on, and I suddenly wanted more than anything to change that. I thought about how it would feel to have the weight of his body on top of me, and the thought made me moan out loud.

He smiled. With his right hand, he touched my cheek. He brushed his thumb over my lips, and it woke something inside of me. Something that had been dormant for too long. It ignited the blood in my veins. It made me ache.

He touched my lips again with the ball of his thumb, and I whimpered.

"You're pure, and sweet, and generous to a fault."

I might have argued if I hadn't been so focused on his caress and on the look in his eyes. He trailed his fingertips down my neck, over my collarbone, making my heart race. Slowly—so slowly—he moved his caress down the center of my chest.

"That day we had ice cream, you put that spoonful in my mouth, and all I could think was, 'If I kissed him now, this is how he would taste.'" He kissed my jaw. "I was so close to kissing you then, but you wouldn't have let me." He kissed my neck. "You have no idea how much I want you."

I didn't understand how it could be true, but at that moment, I didn't care. His touch felt so good. I was fully erect in my shorts. Not only that, I was already terrifyingly close to climax. I wasn't sure how I'd gone from the verge of tears to the brink of orgasm so quickly, but I wanted nothing more than to see where he'd take me.

He stroked my stomach with his fingertips. "You have this amazing skin that's so smooth and white. All I ever think about is touching it." He leaned down and kissed my collarbone. "And tasting it." With agonizing slowness, he moved his finger down my stomach. "You're even softer than I imagined."

I whimpered again, resisting the urge to arch my hips toward him. Somehow, the waiting was better. He circled my navel with his thumb. Trying to fight back the surge in my groin, I rode the waves until I had no choice but to give in to the overwhelming desire to push myself against him.

"You're not second to anybody, Paul. Not in my mind. I think you're beautiful, inside and out."

He moved his hand lower, brushing at the waistband of my briefs, over my hipbone, tickling the sensitive spot where my thigh met my groin, and I shivered. It was the first kiss all over again, except this time it wasn't pretend. It was real. Or at least it felt real, and I never, ever wanted it to stop. It was a fire burning inside me, each caress making me ache, each spot more sensitive than the last. It was the most amazing thing I'd ever experienced.

"I shouldn't be doing this," he said hoarsely. "Not when you're this drunk."

No. Not this again. My eyes snapped open to look up into his, but the expression on his face killed my anger. God, his eyes. Dark and sultry and yet with a hint of reservation in them.

I gave up. "Please," I whispered. "Oh God, El. *Please.*"

He cupped my erection in his hand, and I gasped. El smiled and winked at me. "Who's desperate now?"

Desperate? God yes, I was desperate for him to give me more. He touched the head of my cock through my shorts. I cried out, and as I did, he kissed me, gently touching his tongue to mine. I wrapped my arms around his neck and pulled him down to me, chest to chest, his thigh pressed between my legs, kissing him as if I could somehow give up everything to him and become what he claimed to see.

He nuzzled against my lips, breaking our kiss. "I should make you wait until you're sober—"

"No!"

"But you have no idea how hard it's been to wait this long. I've thought about doing this a hundred times." His warm hand moved on my cock, changing from a caress to a grip. "I feel like I've thought about nothing at all since we met except kissing you and tasting you and touching you and fucking you, or letting you fuck me—"

I moaned, knowing I couldn't last more than another second. "El—"

He kissed me again, cutting off my voice, breaking my control.

One hard stroke.

Two.

That was all it took.

I came, gasping for air, clutching at him as if he were life itself. I forgot about the day, my failures, everything that had brought me to this place. There was only him, so strong and lean, the exotic taste of his mouth, the rough grip of his hand as he stroked me through my orgasm, his gentle kisses on my cheek and brow and jaw as I fought to catch my breath. The hardness of his erection in his jeans, pressed firmly against my thigh.

All at once I was aware of the fact that I'd simply lain there. That I'd come before he'd even undressed.

"I'm sorry," I said.

He smiled and kissed my nose. "Don't be."

The afterglow of my orgasm made me shiver and sigh. I felt limp and heavy and sated and unbelievably sleepy. Even the idea of waking up stuck to my shorts wasn't enough to make me do more than settle in comfortably against his weight. He put his arms around me and sighed against my neck. "I hope you don't hate me for this in the morning."

I hated somebody in the morning, but it wasn't Emanuel. It was whoever had invented the juice of the devil more commonly known as rum.

I woke around five, my head pounding and my stomach in turmoil. El wasn't there, which was fine because I threw up for an hour, eventually giving up and sleeping on the bathroom floor between bouts so I didn't have to move so far to get the job done. When I woke up at nine, the bathroom rug pattern impressed on my face, I finally emerged from the bathroom and collapsed back into bed.

At noon I woke to the beeping sound of my phone announcing a text. It was from El.

Hope you're feeling okay this morning. Sorry I didn't stick around but wasn't sure if you'd want me there or not. I hope you don't think I took advantage of you while you were drunk. Even though I did. Call if you want.

Another text followed. *MoJo says hi and that she didn't take advantage of you at all, so don't take your disgust at me out on her.*

I smiled again, though I bit the inside of my cheek at the same time, trying to quell the upset in my stomach that had nothing to do with too much rum. I felt like I should text back, but I didn't know what to say. Telling myself I'd think of something later, I put the phone down and went to the kitchen to see what food I might be able to keep down.

Except as I searched through my cupboards, full of food instead of useless appliances, I remembered last night. Remembered the way El had smiled at me. The way he'd danced with me. I remembered his touch and the taste of his kiss and the wonderful feeling of being in his arms. I remembered the way he'd touched me and told me I was beautiful inside and out. I remembered feeling amazing. Cherished. Loved.

That feeling was tempered more than a little by the acknowledgment of what exactly I had done and with whom. Specifically, that the whom had been a man.

After my shower, I stood in front of the bathroom mirror, staring into my own eyes. The chipmunk part of my brain was back on its wheel, chattering away about how it didn't matter, how I had been drunk, how it was just messing around. Except that other voice wasn't whispering in the back of my head now. It really wasn't saying anything, but it wasn't muted. It pushed the chipmunk further and further back, calling up memories older than the ones from the night before. Of kissing the neighbor boy, Dean. Of feeling my heart race when he'd breathed against my neck. Of catching sight of boys in the locker room and being turned on—and terrified.

Of being caught by Dean's mom with his hand on my cock, of her screaming, of me begging her not to tell my mom. Of never seeing Dean again after that.

Of being tempted by guys at college but being rescued by Stacey and her willingness to direct my life. Of how the longer I was with Stacey, the less I thought about guys at all until I couldn't even remember having ever liked them.

I stared at myself and had a strange sort of epiphany, or at least something that felt like one, a kind of companion to that unsettled sensation I'd had at El's text, and just like then, I couldn't put it into words. Because it wasn't about words. It was about feelings. It was about wanting. About aching.

About *needing*.

The sensation carried me out of the house and into my car, which seemed to know it was supposed to go to Tucker Pawn, because that's where I ended up. The shop was closed, but the feelings carried me around the side to a door which could only go up to his apartment.

It wasn't until I heard MoJo barking excitedly and El cooing to her as he came down the stairs that I remembered I'd meant to call him, not show up unannounced on a Sunday afternoon. So when he opened the door, I was frozen in fear and mortification and the same emptiness I remembered through a rum haze when he'd told me he needed to take me home.

"Paul." That was all he said, and he seemed surprised, but not exactly excited to see me. Wary, definitely.

I still couldn't speak. I wanted him to smile, to tease me, because he always did. He wasn't now, though. He just looked at me, guarded, unreadable. Unhelpful.

I think I'd arrived believing it would be some kind of movie moment where he'd sweep me into his arms and we'd kissed and everything would work out. The weird part was, I could feel that possibility lurking underneath us, except neither of us were willing to make that leap. Or maybe I was the only one wishing for cheesy violins. Maybe he was hoping I would buy a clue and go away.

He'd wanted me last night, though. That much I remembered. He'd wanted me this morning. But standing here now, looking at him with all his wariness, it was so easy to believe he'd come to his senses. Or that I'd already managed to screw everything up before I even had myself figured out.

It didn't help that I *still* didn't know what to say, what I felt, what I wanted. So with nothing else to offer, I said, "We need to talk."

His expression the same, he nodded. "Probably so." He opened the door.

Then he picked up MoJo and headed up the stairs.

I followed, forgetting I'd ever had a hangover and wishing like hell for a bottle of rum.

CHAPTER 20

El fussed with MoJo as he led Paul into the apartment, trying not to let on how panicked he truly was.

He'd been bouncing off the walls ever since he'd sent the text, alternating between wearing holes in his floorboards and obsessively checking his phone to make sure the ringer was on, that the ringer still worked, that the phone worked, period, that it was loud enough for him to hear even in the bedroom if it rang, and most importantly of all, that Paul hadn't called or texted him and he'd missed it.

Whether it was because Paul appearing at his door wasn't part of his plan or because he'd appeared spouting the four most ominous words in the universe—*we need to talk*—El couldn't say. Maybe it would have been this way on the phone, too. Maybe it had always been destined to head here. Maybe—actually, no maybe about it—he should never have opened this can of worms in the first place.

Except he knew all the way down to the soles of his shoes that he would do this all again in a heartbeat, even if Paul was about to kiss him good-bye. Without so much as a kiss.

Paul, he realized, still hadn't said anything. Glancing over to check, El saw his guest holding up a wall near his small dining table at the edge of the room that was his cooking, living, and eating area. Paul looked as terrified as El felt, all but begging with his eyes to be let out of this conversation.

El let out a huff of air and swallowed a grimace. The hell he would coach Paul through cutting him loose. He plunked down on the corner of the couch and motioned for MoJo to jump up in his lap—a useless gesture, as she was already halfway there. "Have a seat. Tell me what's on your mind."

The only seats available were the recliner, which was practically to El's back the way he was sitting, and the other end of the small couch he already occupied. It depressed the hell out of him when Paul chose to drag a chair over from the table. "I—I'm sorry. I know you said to call."

"It's fine." El smiled, but it felt like something strange and constipated. He gave it up and focused on rubbing behind MoJo's ears. "So. You said we need to talk."

He could practically *feel* Paul's discomfort radiating across the room. "I— Yes. I mean, don't you? About last night? I—" He stammered a moment, and when El gave in and glanced up, Paul's face, neck, and ears were red. "Or maybe you don't. Maybe that was normal for you and no big deal." Paul's eyes weren't closed, but they were focused so hard on a spot on the floor that El figured there'd likely be a hole by the end of the conversation. "It was a big deal for me."

Hell. With a heavy sigh, El displaced MoJo and scooted forward on the couch, bracing his elbows against his knees. "It was for me too. Except it looks like it's upset you, so I'm sorry. Like I said last night, you were drunk, and I knew better. I'm sorry."

"No." Paul's gaze lifted quickly, urgently, then fell to the floor in a new wave of blushing. "I mean—" He began to worry his fingers, tugging at them and bending them into contortions that made El brace himself for the crack of bones. "I was drunk. Very drunk. But I think I remember everything. Including how you tried to get me home, and—" Now his eyes did fall shut, and the wind seemed to go out of him.

"I'm sorry," El whispered, feeling shitty and helpless.

Paul laughed, a strange, tortured sound. "That's . . . that's just it. I don't know that I am."

The weight of dread over El froze and lifted slightly. "Oh?"

The fingers launched back into their contortions. "I've been thinking about it all day. Trying to. Mostly I feel confused and panicked and something else I can't figure out how to describe except that it's why I ended up over here. I mean—I thought I was over this. I hadn't *thought* about this. Not in a long, long time."

"Thought about what?"

Paul was almost sweating. "Being—being—" Those fingers were never going to make it.

"Gay?" El finished for him.

Paul shook his head, then stopped as if he were confused. "Yes—well, I mean, I don't know that I am. All the way, I mean. It's not like I had to talk myself into sex with Stacey."

El could do without hearing that woman's name again, ever. Especially when attached to sex with Paul. "Well, Kinsey didn't make his scale out of nothing."

Paul nodded, blushing a little. "I mean, I've been with guys before. Well, one. Sort of. One guy, one girl. I guess it's never been a big deal to me—I've always been attracted to both. But it's easier to be with women."

Biting back comments about how much hell Stacey had put Paul through, El held still and waited. Paul, however, merely hunched over himself, his breathing coming fast and shallow. El gave up and scooted all the way to the end of the couch, reaching for Paul but stopping short of touching his knee. "Paul."

Paul plowed on. "Sometimes I wonder how much of being with Stacey was taking the easy way out. It seems stupid now, as stupid as everything else I've tried to do, pretending to be someone I'm not. I don't even have some great reason, like my parents are religious zealots who protest gay funerals or something. Not even close. It just . . . it was never safe to be with men. And I didn't *hate* girls. I never sat down and reasoned it out, but I think some part of me decided why make a fuss? Why make life hard?" His hands tightened into each other, his whole body tensing as his voice rose. "Now it's all awake, all those old feelings I thought I'd put away. They're all right here, and I don't want to be this, don't want the complicated way, but I don't want to say no, and you probably think I'm an idiot, which I am, but I can't turn it off, I don't want to try, and that was amazing and I want to do it again, but I—"

At *you probably think I'm an idiot*, El started moving; at *I don't want to try*, he knelt in front of Paul, who was hyperventilating and talking as fast as a rabid auctioneer; at *I want to do it again*, he allowed himself one moment to savor the words, and then he took Paul's face in his hands and stopped the flow of chatter with a kiss.

It was a sweet kiss, a slow kiss, meant to gentle Paul and possibly get a little air back *into* his lungs instead of letting it all fall out in a rush of words, but it didn't stay that way long. Paul whimpered, rested trembling hands on El's shoulders, and El groaned back, teasing Paul's lips open to deepen the kiss.

"I'll stop if you want," he whispered, sliding his hands down to Paul's waist. "Just tell me what you want."

"I don't know." Paul leaned hard into El, his body clearly not suffering from indecision. "I just . . . I just . . . I . . ."

El placed a kiss on Paul's chin. "It's me. Okay? I'm not going to hurt you, and I'm not going to laugh. Tell me what you want. What you need." He nuzzled his way back to that sweet, soft mouth. "Let me give it to you."

Paul's swallow was audible. "I'm sorry. I feel like a little kid. I probably sound like one. That can't be attractive."

"I promise you're very attractive. And nothing like a kid." El's fingers dipped into Paul's waistband, then paused. "We can just talk, Paul. I don't want you to feel like I'm pushing you into anything. I've done more than enough of that already."

Paul's gaze fixed on El, hesitant and heated at once. "Maybe... maybe I want to be pushed."

El allowed himself a moment to drink that in too. Then he pulled Paul onto his lap, nudged the chair aside, and kissed Paul without holding anything back while he pushed him with surety of purpose to the floor.

Paul's needy gasps and clutching hands spurred him on. "Did you *really* want me from the moment you saw me?" Paul whispered between heated kisses.

"Yeah." El couldn't figure out where he wanted to touch Paul first, so he kept his hands moving, shoving aside clothing, seeking skin. "I want you now. Tell me what's too far, Paul. Tell me right now."

"Nothing. I want all of it."

Remembering the dazed, frightened look he'd been treated to at the bottom of the stairs, El mentally wrote several activities off despite what Paul had said. "I don't want you to freak out afterward." His throat threatened to close in self-defense, but he shoved through the blockage and pressed on. "Because I don't just want to make love to you today. I want to be with you, Paul." That was as much as he could get out. He went back to making love to Paul's neck.

Paul arched into him, tilting his head to make the job easier. "Like . . . a boyfriend?"

It took three swallows to get the lump down. "If that's what you want." When Paul tensed, El ached. "Or something else. Or nothing. Whatever you want."

Paul's breath shuddered out of him. "I— maybe? It's— I can't even say it to myself without panicking. I don't even think I can say what I am—what this means—out loud." He leaned his forehead against El. "I don't think I'd be a good one just now."

But maybe later. The idea terrified and thrilled El at once. He lifted his head to grin at Paul. "You take your time with that."

"I can't believe you want me," Paul said, cheeks staining again.

If El could have purred, he would have. "Let me show you how much I do.

CHAPTER 21

I was going to have sex.

With a man.

With El.

The thought kept banging around in my head like a ball bearing as he pushed me backward into his bedroom, kissing me all the way there like he could only get air by molesting my mouth. I felt jumbled, wanting to give him whatever he wanted, desperate for it, but panicked too. *This was it.* I wasn't exactly sure what *it* was, but I was at some kind of crossroads, a big X in the middle of my personal road, going left instead of right in a way I'd never gone before. I was fairly sure we were going to go further than I'd even thought about going with Dean. I wanted to go there. The theme to *Star Trek* played idiotically in my head: *To boldly go where no Paul has gone before.*

El might fuck me. El might put his dick in my ass.

The very thought made my limbs shake with want and my insides curdle with fear.

His hands tugged at the hem of my shirt, making my belly cave and quiver. I gasped when his fingers skimmed my skin as he pulled the garment away, looking dizzily into his gaze and finding my own lust mirrored there.

He really wanted me. I reached out to touch his face, half afraid he'd vanish on contact.

Sharp barking broke the spell, and El looked down, laughing before pulling away to crouch and pet MoJo. "Hey, sweetheart. Let Daddy get a little loving, okay?"

MoJo continued to bark eagerly, and enough of my lust faded for logic to rise to the occasion. "Give her a toy she loves, something that will keep her busy."

El grimaced, then went to his closet, fishing around on the floor. He came back with a beat-up sneaker that had MoJo all but doing cartwheels of joy. After tossing it into the living room and watching MoJo run after it, he shut the bedroom door. "I'm going to have to start buying shoes more often if I want to get laid on a regular basis, I can see that."

The center of my chest felt funny at *laid on a regular basis,* but I squelched the joy, cautioning myself it wasn't just me. "Find her a special toy and let her only have it when you want her to leave you alone."

El took me back into his arms, sliding a hand over my naked chest while the other teased at the waistband of my jeans. "As often as I'd like to be alone with you, I'm going to need a full armory of special toys."

I didn't know what to do with that, so I moved in closer, brushing against his shirt. I wanted it gone, wanted nothing between us, and I tugged at his hem, frustrated to find it tucked into his jeans. Chuckling, he let go of me long enough to peel the shirt away.

Our flesh came together, his dark against my light. I had one moment to appreciate the contrast before lust took over, at which point he could have turned purple and I wouldn't have cared. I was too busy attacking his mouth and moving us backward onto the bed.

I felt chaotic, swept up and consumed by what we were doing while fearing it at the same time. *You'll be gay if you do this,* the chipmunk warned. *If you let him fuck you, there's no going back. You'll be gay.*

I wanted to argue with that assessment because I could see the logic holes from here, but logic had never won over the chipmunk, and the part of me that could have argued was too busy lifting my hips so El could more easily dispose of my jeans. I lay naked on the bed, breath coming hard and fast as I took in the beautiful sight of El hovering over me. He wasn't hairy, not at all, except for the most delicious treasure trail leading down to his cock, which stood brown and erect and eager to meet me. I smelled him too, a sharp, slightly sweaty male scent that reminded me of locker rooms and sleepovers. I remembered my best friend complaining of the stink, remembered thinking it was actually pretty delicious but that I'd clearly best keep that thought to myself. That smell was back now: a little sweat, a little spice, a little something undefinable that made me dizzy.

El smiled at me, leaned forward, and the smell overwhelmed me enough to make me close my eyes and open my mouth on a silent inhale, tasting him on the air. Only for a second, though, because then his mouth found mine, the intensity of his kiss a jolt sending me into a land of nothing but sensation before he broke away to slide down my body. Propped up on my elbows, I watched in a disoriented haze as his dark head bobbed up and down on me, over and over until finally I caught his hair in a desperate fist.

"Stop or I'm going to come," I whispered.

He smiled around the tip of my cock, a gesture that nearly put me over the edge by itself. "I thought that was the idea."

The chipmunk came babbling back in a rush, but I shoved it aside all by myself this time. "I want more."

The way El's gaze darkened made me shiver. "How much more?"

"I told you. All of it." Gathering up all my courage, I said. "I want you to fuck me."

Why did he seem surprised? I would have cringed, except he was clearly eager too. "You don't have to do that."

"I want to," I reassured him, even though my ass was clenching at the very thought.

He caught the tip of my penis in a quick suckle-kiss before he smiled. "You know, they don't have a badge for anal sex in the Gay Scouts. It doesn't make you any more or less."

"I know that," I said, but too quickly, because I really didn't.

The truth must have shown on my face, because he shifted to lie beside me, leaning on his elbow as he spoke. "Some guys live for it. Some refuse to do it ever. Some save it for a kind of rite of passage in a relationship. Some will do it in the back room of a bar."

"What do you do?"

God, but I loved that wry smile. "A little of everything except the back room of a bar."

That was good, I decided. As exciting as the back room of a bar was in theory, I wasn't sure I was up for it in practice. "What do you want to do right now? And don't say whatever I want to do," I added quickly, because I knew that's what he'd tell me if I didn't disallow it.

He seemed to consider his options for a moment, his hand idly stroking my thigh as he did so. Finally his gaze met mine, those beautiful dark eyes bare and honest, more so than I thought I'd ever seen them. "I want you. I want to fuck you. I want you to fuck me. I want to rim you until you come on my sheets. I want to rub off together in the shower. I want to watch you masturbate. I want you to jack my cock. I want you to blow me. I want to blow you again. I want to do you in a chair. I want to do you in the bed with you facing me. I want to pound into you from behind. I want you to pound into me from behind."

Forget the blowjob. I was going to spill just listening to him. "That all sounds good," I whispered.

But El wasn't done. He kept speaking, and if I thought he'd been naked for the first soliloquy, he peeled back the skin on his chest for what came next.

"I want to lie in bed with you and listen to a rainstorm come in over the mountains. I want to find out what you eat for breakfast. I want you to stop by the shop because you want to see me, not because you have some crap from your ex you want to unload."

I stared at him, recognizing the quiet terror behind his confession because I felt it in myself, though I didn't quite get why. "No, you don't," I said at last.

He relaxed back into amusement. "Is that so?"

I wasn't relaxed. I felt even more panicked, in fact. "Why would you want me like that?" When he stiffened up again, I felt compelled to keep talking. "You're saying you want to date me. Why?"

"I'm trying to decide if you're insulting yourself or me or both with the assumption that I wouldn't want to date you. Or is that your way of politely telling me you want to fuck me but not date me?"

Was that what I was saying? I had no idea. I propped myself up further, regarding him soberly, a little desperately. "There's nothing special about me. And as a boyfriend—I'm bad in general, but I've never been with a man. Somebody like you . . ." I trailed off, unsure of how to finish that without sounding completely pathetic.

Crawling over me, El pushed me back into the mattress, rubbing our naked cocks against one another, rousing them back to full life. "Somebody like me wants to fuck you, and he also wants to hang out with you. Like we've already been doing, but without excuses, just admitting that we want to because we like it. Think you can handle that?"

My hands had found their way to his shoulders, and I dug my fingernails into his skin as I thrust up against him "Yes. Oh God, El. Please—please, fuck me."

He laughed. "Since you ask so nicely . . ."

We rubbed together like that a few minutes, kissing harder and harder until we were both panting and on the edge of coming, at which point he turned me over and answered my unasked question about what he'd meant by rimming me. It turned out that meant kneeling behind me, spreading my cheeks open, and alternately licking my hole and fucking it with his tongue. Before we were done, I'd ripped the sheets from his bed down to the mattress pad, wadding them into my fists and coating them in sweat. He kept me from coming, squeezing my balls just enough to keep the edge away, and when I was nothing but jelly-bodied from head to toe, he flipped me over, reached for something at his bedside, and covered my mouth with another kiss.

I hadn't put anything inside me, ever, so his slicked-up finger came as quite a shock—so much so that I broke the kiss. Our gazes met and held as his single finger pushed carefully but insistently inside me.

His voice was thick and rough as he asked, "Want me to stop?"

Yes. No. I shut my eyes and gripped his shoulders. "Oh God." His finger stilled, and I chased after it wantonly. "Please," I whispered.

His mouth found mine again, briefly this time before exploring my chin and neck, distracting me as he continued to push in and out of me. I clutched at him, gasping and babbling, especially when I felt an additional stretch and knew he'd added another finger.

I felt his fingers turning inside me, a sensation so strange and erotic at the same time that I could only lie there absorbing, at best pushing back against his thrusts at times to try to take him deeper. Sometimes he would brush against something deep inside me, sending light waves of pleasure so hard through my system it made my jaw ache. *Prostate*, I thought absently, then gave over to gasping and moaning, his name, God's, whoever would listen. The oddness of being penetrated evaporated, and I knew only pleasure, yearning for more.

When we were both hard and desperate, he pulled away and headed for the bathroom. This confused me until I saw him emerge with a small foil packet in his hand, which he held up to his eyes, squinting at it as he flipped it over a few times. Eventually he stopped, shoulders sagging in relief, and came back to me. At my quizzical look, he pursed his lips, looking embarrassed.

"Checking the expiration date," he confessed.

Why that made me smile, I don't know. "Are we good?"

"Very," he replied as he sheathed himself in latex.

Though I'd thought I was accustomed to having something in my ass by now, when I felt his cockhead at my entrance I still paused, holding my breath. El caught my gaze, and I blushed. "Sorry. I feel like a virgin."

El smiled his sideways smile. "Touched for the very first time," he sang, then pushed, ever so slightly, inside.

I shut my eyes on a soft gasp, lifting my hips to encourage him deeper. Inch by careful inch he claimed me, until I felt his groin against my skin, his cock fully encased inside me.

I was a virgin no more.

He took me carefully at first, moving slowly, letting me get used to him, bending down at times to kiss me, to tease my nipples. Even before I started to tug at him, though, his control began to slip, and in those moments before I gave in to my own desire, I felt him slide into his: for the first time, really, except that moment when he'd confessed that he wanted to date me. I watched El Rozal give up his cynicism and control and even his niceties and simply lose himself in fucking me, no longer giving me pleasure but taking his own.

Somehow that made me feel safe enough to do the same. I stopped thinking about what was happening and what it meant. I took my cock in my hand, and as El let go, I followed.

I've had sex with a man. With El. I smiled to myself as post-sex lethargy seized me.

I couldn't wait to do it again.

El lay awake in the dark, on his side on top of the covers, as he watched Paul sleep.

They hadn't done everything on El's sexual list, but they'd made some serious headway. He'd get hard in the shower for a month just thinking about what they'd done in there, and his recliner was now officially an erogenous zone. Takeout subs would probably give him a boner for the foreseeable future, as well.

He still felt a well of panic whenever he thought about the other things he'd confessed, and the fact that Paul hadn't ever exactly said, "Why yes, I'd love to date you, and aren't you so sweet to ask that way," or anything remotely Hallmark-like, wasn't helping his case. Where the fuck that had come from, he didn't know, but he wished he could stuff the conversation back. He felt too raw, too exposed.

This wasn't supposed to happen. Hadn't Denver pointed out that he'd thrown his hat into the ring of a game he couldn't win? Wasn't this exact situation what he'd always sworn he'd avoid?

A rustle and a brush of hair against his toes was his only warning before something lapped at his feet. "Come here, girl," El whispered, and MoJo promptly scurried over, trading up to lick his face.

El shut his eyes, settled back into his pillow, and gave himself over to her ministrations.

CHAPTER 22

I'm gay.

The words resonated in my head all the way home late that night, as I went to sleep, and when I woke up the next morning. I woke up early too, so early I decided to walk to the office. I swung by Mocha Springs Eternal and got an egg sandwich and a latte, eating out on the sidewalk tables because it was a beautiful morning. I couldn't think about that, though. All I could think about was, *I'm gay.*

I don't know if I was trying to get used to it or what. I still wasn't entirely sure that's what I was—gay, or bi? I didn't know, and I wasn't sure it mattered. The idea wasn't making the pit of my stomach feel like a big hole anymore, but it still felt like my throat was stopped up with my heart, which beat so hard it tried to come out my ears. All I knew was I felt strange, like I'd woken up in new skin. Or with some new door open letting in a breeze that alternately excited me and made me panic.

I'm gay. Or bi. Or something.

I'm gay.

I walked in the front door of the office. Nick stood behind the counter, checking something on my computer. When he saw me, he smiled. "Hey, Paul. How are you this fine Monday?"

"I'm gay," I replied.

Out loud. I'd said it out loud. I froze, the heart-in-throat feeling so intense I thought I'd pass out.

Nick blinked a few times, then winked at me as he grinned. "Congratulations." He turned back to the monitor. "Just printing something and then I'll be out of your hair."

Eventually I was able to move, but my legs felt like jelly as I came behind the counter. "Sorry. I—I don't know why I blurted that out."

"I think a little more blurting things out would be good for you, Paul, especially things as important as that." He hit a few keystrokes and stood up, stretching and grimacing at his watch. "Brooke already called in. I probably should have out-and-out fired her, but . . ." His gaze slid to me. "Well, to be honest, I wanted to talk to you before I did anything."

I was still reeling from my confession, and I couldn't keep up with such an abrupt conversational shift. "Me?"

"Yes, you." He leaned against the file cabinet and gave me an almost scolding look. "I've been waiting for you to suggest this yourself, but clearly you need a bit of a nudge. What would you say to taking Brooke's place?"

"Sure. I never mind filling in."

Nick's smile lifted at the corners. "I mean taking her place permanently, Paul. How would you like to be my vet tech?"

I'm pretty sure my jaw fell open. "Me?"

"Yes, you. I know you did at least some vet school, so you have to have most of the classes for the associate degree already. It might seem weird, going back for an undergraduate degree when you already have one, but really, I think that will make it that much easier for you, having played the game once before. I'll be able to give you more to do if you go back for the full four-year program, but even that you should be able to complete with a patch job. If you aren't comfortable with student loans, we can negotiate some kind of advance or I can help you look into scholarships."

When I remained speechless, he laughed and nudged me with his elbow. "Come on, say yes. I don't want to hire another flake. I want to hire you."

I didn't know what to say. Between El telling me—and showing me—he wanted me and now Nick offering not just to hire me as a tech but also to help me go back to school for the official degree, I wondered if I was dreaming. Next thing I knew I'd be winning the Curb Appeal contest. This wasn't my life. Things like this didn't happen to me.

And yet, it appeared that at least for now, they did.

"Okay," I said at last, and Nick clapped me on the back.

"Great. Put out an ad for a new receptionist, and as soon as we get you a replacement, we can start your technician training in earnest. Meanwhile, put in your application for the fall semester at East Centennial, and we can talk about how you want to pay for it over lunch."

I told El about my new job when he came over to my house after closing up the shop for the night. It seemed a little early to me for him to be closing, but we were so focused on the job thing, I forgot to ask why.

"He acted like he'd been waiting for me to volunteer for the job," I told El as we maneuvered *Detroit Daisy* to the back of the house. He'd told me he'd be over in a few days to pick it up with his friend's truck. He seemed oddly happy about it, too. MoJo was also filled with joy, but it seemed to be more about a pair of butterflies that kept dancing around her head while she wrapped her lead chain round the tree we'd tied her to.

"Probably he figured out that waiting for you to realize he wanted you would mean waiting until Doomsday. Shit, this is crazy heavy."

I stopped, peering around the sculpture at El. "What do you mean, he'd wait until Doomsday for me to figure it out?"

"Because that's how you are, Paul. The last one to know when someone wants you." When I opened my mouth to protest, he rode over my objection, nodding to Bill's yard. "That girl over there is the same one you went to lunch with the other day, right?"

How did he know I'd been to lunch with Lorraine? "Yeah, why?"

"She keeps casting these longing looks your way, but they don't seem to register with you at all. I bet she thinks you're not interested, but I'm betting you don't even have a clue that she *is* interested, do you?"

My eyes widened as I glanced over to where Lorraine huddled with Bill over a flat of annuals. "Lorraine is interested? In me?" I frowned. "No. She's picking favorites for the contest, is all."

"Like I said. Doomsday." He slid a hand around my waist and brushed a kiss on my cheek.

I glanced over at Lorraine a lot after that, trying to decide if El was right. We were doing some more work together on my yard, taking out Stacey's edging and putting in a few things El had found at the shop, some of them actual lawn ornaments, some of them nothing more than interesting items he seemed to believe would help my cause. The jewel-colored, glass-studded birdbath was great, but I wasn't sure about the old bicycle until he had it propped up against the side of the house in front of an old window, with, of all things, some broken pots. But once it was all arranged, it didn't look too bad.

"It'll be better with a few plants in front of it, and maybe some pea gravel. My abuela has some plants that need thinning, and my sister has a pile of rocks on a slab in her backyard from some project that never got finished. She needs those gone anyway, so I'll bring them over tomorrow night. Hey. That reminds me." He tucked a hand in his pocket, looking almost nervous. "What are you doing on the Fourth?"

"My mom will be in town. She'll be here on Wednesday, actually. Why?"

"No reason," El said, sounding relieved, and turned away.

I didn't press him because I was too busy realizing I'd have to tell my mother I was gay. Or did I? Maybe I could do it the next time she visited. Unless El kissed me or something in front of her. Would he do that, though?

What were we doing, anyway? Dating? We weren't boyfriends, we'd said, but . . . I thought of what we'd done together the night before, and blood pooled in my groin.

How would we be able to do anything at all with my mother here?

"Slow down, tiger," El said, laughter in his voice. "You're going to short your brain out with all that thinking."

"Sorry." I relaxed from the crouch I'd been holding in front of a flowerbed and sat hard on the ground, my brain still moving as fast as ever. "This is all just . . . overwhelming."

"This what?"

"This." I gestured between the two of us. "Us. Being together. Like we were last night."

El raised an eyebrow at me. "Why?"

I swallowed hard. "I just . . . I still have a hard time believing it, I guess. That you would . . . want me." That *anybody* would, but I wouldn't be pathetic and admit that.

"That seems to be a theme with you, not knowing people want you— in lots of ways." He cocked his head to the side. "I wonder how many people have tried to get your attention, only to wander off in despair of ever achieving it."

The thought startled me, and I endured a few terrible moments of combing through my memories, wondering where he might have been right, wondering how I'd ever find out.

He chuckled. "They just have no staying power, in my opinion. Anyway, their loss is my gain."

I looked at him levelly. "Because *you* want me." I felt silly saying it out loud, but somehow, the moment seemed to call for reassurance.

He leaned in close, drawing my earlobe into his mouth before whispering, "Yes."

I was dizzier now, but in a very good way. "So that means you want to . . ."

He chuckled and nuzzled my ear again. "Take you to bed? Yeah, Paul. I do." The kiss he placed on my temple was so light it made my stomach fill with butterflies. "Would that be okay with you?"

"Yes," I whispered.

I thought he would laugh again, but he didn't. Instead, he put his hand on my thigh and squeezed. "Would you like to go to bed with me right now?"

"Yes," I said quickly, eagerly, and the next thing I knew, I'd been lifted to my feet, and I followed El as he led me inside by the hand.

I glanced at Lorraine again as El let go of me to rescue MoJo, and I kept my eye on her as we rounded the corner to the front door. She had a very odd look on her face, and I felt my face heat as I realized what she'd seen.

It dawned on me that being with El in any way at all truly would mean I'd be telling everyone I was gay. Not just Nick, but my neighbors and everyone. Random people who saw us kissing or smiling at each other. People in the supermarket, maybe. My mom—if not this week, then eventually.

I'd have to tell Stacey.

I didn't know what to think about this. I didn't *want* to think about this, but something told me there was no way El would keep us as a secret. Or if he would, he wouldn't like it, which would almost be worse. Thinking about announcing it, though, made it all so real, breaking the chipmunk out of his paralysis to ask me how I knew I really was gay, or whatever, how I didn't know this wasn't some kind of hallucination and I'd come out as gay but then not be gay later and wouldn't that be a mess?

And what if Stacey came back again, this time for good?

El's fingers teased my wrist, and I remembered all the things we'd done the night before, that we were about to do all over again and maybe more. I remembered that I didn't want Stacey anymore, even if she wanted me. I stopped wondering about whether or not I was really gay, and I forgot, at least for the moment, that I was supposed to care.

CHAPTER 23

A s El followed Paul inside, he thought about the pensiveness he'd seen on his lover's face and acknowledged they were in a kind of honeymoon phase, a happy little bubble before the other shoe fell and reality set in. Even if Paul wasn't voicing his concerns out loud, Paul's lack of a poker face was on par with his obliviousness about who was interested in him. As Denver would say, Strawberry Shortcake hadn't even begun to grapple with the complexities of coming out. El would lay even odds that Paul was deep in the "maybe it's a mistake and I'm confused, not gay" stage. He didn't want to think about Paul being bi, which was probably unfair, but man, he wanted to hear Paul say, "Stacey was a mistake. I only want you." Which could happen either way, but boy it would feel good to give the woman that kind of kick in the teeth.

Okay, so he was an asshole on that count. Bi, gay—whatever way Paul went, he had quite a road ahead of him.

El thought about telling his own coming-out story: how he knew in high school but kept it on the down-low until he'd graduated, how he'd sweated bullets over telling his family, how they'd cried when he had. That left him feeling far too vulnerable, though, so he considered offering up the tale of losing his virginity, of the terrifying and wonderful experience of being pinned down on a hotel bed by a biker daddy. He thought about simply assuring Paul this was a journey, that he should take his time. He wanted to reassure Paul and emphasize that he shouldn't let anyone rush him, not even El.

When he came into the bedroom after setting MoJo up with some water and her favorite toys in the kitchen, though, one look at his lover on the edge of the bed, shoes off and bare toes curling around each other protectively as he hunched his shoulders, his eyes radiating the now-heady cocktail of want and terror and naked lust, El found he couldn't say anything at all. He simply tugged his T-shirt over his head, kicked off his shoes, and reached for his fly.

He loved the way Paul's gaze raked him, greedily taking in every inch of flesh as it appeared. Paul's hands echoed the path of the denim, fingers ghosting over El's flesh as Paul's lusty gaze burned. "Your skin is amazing. It's like the color of coffee with just the right amount of cream."

El smiled and let his own hands sink into that beautiful red-brown hair. "And you're Snow White, perfect porcelain skin. Except for where you have those adorable freckles. Then of course there's this delicious strawberry hair."

Normally that would have made Paul blush, but he seemed too fixated on El's abdomen. His lips parted, his tongue stealing out to wet them. "I just want to lick you," he whispered.

Inside his briefs, El's cock twitched with a surge of arousal. "Go right ahead."

Paul's gaze, drunk with lust instead of rum, lifted to El's. For long moments they regarded each other, El daring, Paul . . . well, El didn't know what Paul was doing.

Paul's pink tongue darted out and traced a circle around El's belly button. Their eyes stayed locked the entire time.

It took everything El had, though, to keep his stomach muscles from flexing, to keep from grabbing Paul's head and pulling him close, to not groan and drag Paul's head to his nipples or his cock and beg him to suck. It was delicious torture, watching Paul explore and being the terrain on which he did so.

When the licks turned to nips and cool fingers tugged the elastic of El's briefs down, freeing his fully erect cock, he shuddered, tightened his grip on Paul's hair, and held on as Paul took his cock firmly in hand.

When El found himself longing to guide Paul's greedy fingers around to the back, he drew away with a kiss, padded naked to the bag he'd brought over and left by the closet, and came back with a tube of lube, which he handed to Paul. "Use it if you want to," he said, directing Paul's hand to the crack of his own ass, which had begun to ache with yearning for what he hoped was coming.

"You—you'd let me—" Paul trailed off, clearly embarrassed, but he had lust in his gaze.

"Fuck me? Yeah." El pressed Paul's fingers directly against his hole. "Let you? I'll beg you, if you want."

When Paul's grip pulled El open, something deep, deep inside him let go, let want and desire flood through his whole body. Paul, oblivious to this, stared at El's eager cock as his fingers played tentatively at El's ass. "I thought . . . I figured—well, that you'd want to do me again."

"Oh, I do. Believe me. But I'd love this too." The fingers at his back door got braver, knocking his cock against Paul's neck. "That's the fun of gay sex, you know. Everybody gets to try everything, if they want to."

The fingers exploring El faltered, and Paul ducked his head. "Sorry. I'm still . . ."

"Getting used to hearing the word *gay* attached to you and the sex you might have?" When Paul flinched, El stroked his hair. He should have brought up the bi possibility, but he could only manage, "It's okay, baby. I understand."

"It's all so new still," Paul whispered. His fingers weren't moving at all now. None of him was, except for the shallow rise and fall of his chest as he drew nervous breaths. "It feels like a dream, like I'll wake up."

God, yes. "It's okay."

"I want this." Paul gripped El's cheeks. "I do. But I don't want—well, what if this *is* a dream? I mean, what if I'm not? What if I'm . . . curious, or whatever?"

"It's okay." That reassurance was a lie, but El made himself say it anyway. It wasn't okay, but he'd have to find a way to make it that way. Sliding his hands to Paul's face, El tipped his lover's mouth up for a long, slow kiss. By the end of it, he had Paul on his back while he fumbled with the other man's fly. No sooner did he have that beautiful cock free, though, than he was the one flat on the mattress, Paul undressing with shaking hands before crushing their bodies together, catching his own long, thin cock with El's thicker one, sliding their heads together, arching against El's chest, gasping into his ear.

El nipped Paul's jaw and whispered, "Fuck me, baby."

He loved the way Paul groaned and fumbled for the lube. He pulled his own knees up, giving Paul's slicked fingers access, gasping when the tip of Paul's index finger breached him. In stuttering whispers, he coached his lover through the mechanics of anal sex, of stretching and coaxing muscles, of where he'd tucked the condoms into his bag. He helped Paul's trembling fingers navigate the condom, though his own hands weren't exactly steady either.

He sucked in his breath, both from the pain and the catch in his heart when Paul entered him, because El's gaze never left his lover's face. He caught the wonder there, mixed with lust, peppered liberally with euphoria and the triumph of sex, real sex, of fucking done right, of figuring out that the jigsaw puzzle pieces really could line up, of discovering there wasn't anything in the world like being encased in the tight, dry heat of another man's ass.

When Paul began to move, El let his eyes close, let his ankles wrap around Paul's waist, his arms around the slim barrel of Paul's chest. He let his body open all the way as he took Paul inside him, as the rhythm became deeper and harder and faster, until his lover tensed over and inside him, preparing to fly. Without opening his eyes, El slipped a hand down between them to help himself along, and he caught the wave too, letting go of absolutely everything as he came, including the lie that if Paul did close the door on this for fear of what it meant or for any reason at all, it wasn't going to burn El like nothing ever had before.

CHAPTER 24

I wasn't sure if it was pent-up lust or the need to get as much of El as I could before my mother arrived, but the days before her flight landed in Grand Junction saw us together almost all the time I wasn't working. We had plenty of—at least for me—inventive sex, but we hung out a lot too, making dinner and watching mindless TV together.

It was great, and I tried to enjoy myself. I couldn't shake the feeling, though, that any second now it could all turn, that something would make this beautiful moment end.

One night the lights flickered while we were making spaghetti, and when the stove snapped as I turned a burner off, El got very concerned. "It shouldn't do that."

"I know. I've called the landlord I don't know how many times."

He had the top of the stove lifted up before I got done speaking, and he wouldn't eat until he'd checked all the wires. Eventually he was convinced my kitchen wouldn't go up in flames the next time I made lunch, and after filling our bellies, we went back to bed, even though it was still light outside.

It wasn't when we went to sleep, though.

Stacey and I hadn't been inventive at all. It was missionary or bust most of the time, and in hindsight I was so busy worrying that she could get off that I mostly came and went, so to speak, during the final act. Not with El. Even when El wasn't sucking me off or touching me or kissing me, everything turned me on, and everything felt like it was about me. Tonight he started by teasing me with his fingers as he kissed me, sliding my knee up onto his thigh and slicking me up with some lube. When his index finger speared me to the hilt, I grabbed at his shoulders.

Then he brushed my prostate, and I *bit* his shoulder.

He leaned over me and reached into the drawer. I told myself it wouldn't hurt as much this time, that I wouldn't be as sore after. But before there was any telltale crinkle of foil, something pushed up against me, something cold and hard. When it pushed inside me, I gasped.

When it moved inside me, I moaned.

"Like that, baby?" El whispered, smiling against my lips before he swallowed my next sound with a deep kiss. A dildo, I guess, that's what he'd put inside me, and yes, I did like it. It felt a little weird, but it also felt very, very good, especially when it almost pulled out and went all the way back in again. Pretty soon I was panting and gripping El's shoulders, not because I was in pain but because I wanted him to push the dildo into me a lot harder.

He didn't. He pulled it out and laid me flat on my back, drawing my legs up to drape over his shoulders. His gaze held mine as that foil sound finally came. He held it while he pushed my legs higher and moved against me.

He held it as he pressed his cock up against my hole, as he breached me and buried himself deep, deep inside.

I couldn't decide what I liked more, feeling El inside me or watching him roll his hips, his body bumping hard against the back of my thighs as he slid in and out of me. I'd never felt so exposed and vulnerable and yet so powerful and safe all at the same time.

It felt, really, like sex was supposed to be.

He stayed over at my house again the night before my mom was due to arrive, and this time we had sex until we literally couldn't anymore. I fucked him over the back of a chair. He blew me on the couch. We rubbed against each other in the shower and nearly killed ourselves slipping on the wet tiles, then got out and finished the job on the mat, me behind him again as MoJo watched with her head cocked in confusion from the door, making us laugh. We kissed and blew each other in the bed. And as a sort of last hurrah in the morning, El bent me in half and made love to my mouth with his as he pumped inside me one last time.

He lay in the bed after, sated and smug as he watched me getting dressed.

"Bring your mom by the shop," he told me. "You can decide when you get there whether or not you want to tell her I fucked you up the ass before you went to the airport."

I smiled to myself as I fished through my jeans for my wallet and keys. When I stood, though, I froze as I saw El sitting up in bed, holding Stacey's ring in his hand.

"What are you doing?" I asked, probably a little sharper than I should have.

He raised an eyebrow at me. "I was going to appraise it for you. Figured you'd need a down payment for those vet tech classes." When I didn't say anything, the smile at the corner of his mouth died. "Unless, of course, you want to check if Stacey wants another go."

He was angry, and I knew he had a right to be. What reason did I have to hold onto the ring, especially now? Even if I did, how awful did it look to say no, I didn't want to hock it just yet, when I had to say that to the man I'd made almost constant love to for three days?

It looked awful, yes. Yet the idea of that ring leaving my bedside, of everything being that completely utterly *over*—not just my relationship with her but my whole heterosexual life as I'd known it—felt ten times worse than the cold I could see creeping into El's face. I held out my hands, placating. "Please—you're right, I should sell it, and I will. Just . . . not today, okay?"

"Sure." El tossed the ring back in the dish by my beside, hard enough that it bounced twice before it clattered into a resting place. He pushed himself out of bed and reached for his clothes. "Come on, MoJo. Time to go home."

"El." I reached for his arm, but he moved away from my touch and pulled his shirt on in one deft motion. "*El*. Please. Come on. This is still new to me. I'm still not sure exactly what I am."

I wasn't sure it was possible, but he closed up even more at that. "Whatever."

"Give me a day, even. Just a little time to wrap my head around it all."

"Take as many days as you want," El shot back, and stepped into his jeans.

Panic and fear whipped up like wildfire, and the chipmunk stood in the middle of the blaze, unsure of what he should be worrying about first. "I thought you said I should take my time. That we could go slow."

"Absolutely." He grabbed his bag and whistled. "MoJo, come on, girl."

I followed him into the living room, panicking full-on now, jealous of the dog as he cuddled her close and let her lick his face. He was still rigid, clearly not intending to spare even one more glance at me. "If we can go slow, then why are you so mad?"

He sighed but didn't turn around, didn't look at me. "I'm not." He did look at me then, and he gave me the most flimsy, fake smile I'd ever seen from him. "I'll see you later."

Then he left.

I stood in my living room a long time, feeling like I should go after him, feeling like I should apologize, feeling like I had to do something, anything, to make his anger go away. To get him back. To get us both back to where we'd been. Except if giving up the ring was the only way I could do that—well, I just couldn't do that. Not yet.

I didn't know what that said about me, and I didn't want to look too hard. At anything right now, actually.

I went back to my bedroom, tucked the ring far into the back of my bedside drawer where no one would see it, and then I went to work, determined to lose myself in my new training until it was time to get my mother from the airport.

CHAPTER 25

El would have skipped laundry night, but canceling without a real excuse would have raised more suspicion than showing up and letting Denver ask questions. He tried his only hope for an out, though, calling Rosa to see if she needed any more help getting ready for the party.

She didn't, because Noah had been over when El had been playing lovey-dovey with Paul, and he hadn't just finished the cleaning, he'd appeared with a brand-new patio set. Complete with umbrella. In Rosa's favorite color.

And yet Rosa still talked about going out shopping for a new guy.

"Whoa," Denver said when El came through the door of the laundry, oblivious, perpetually happy MoJo in tow. "Trouble in paradise?"

"Stuff it," El snapped, tossing the end of the leash at him. "Watch her, will you? I'm going to go smoke."

"Hey." Frowning, almost glaring, Denver scooped up MoJo and scratched behind her ears. "What the fuck's gotten into you?"

"Nothing." El bit the word so hard it bled. "Nothing's gotten into me. Can you watch the fucking dog or not?"

Denver lifted MoJo, his big hands making such a cradle for the little dog she probably thought she was on some kind of shelf. "Daddy's got something sideways up his ass, pumpkin. You want to tell Uncle Denver what it is?"

El stormed out the door, went around the corner to the dark of the alley, and smoked until his lungs were practically butter.

His clothes were sorted and loaded into the machines when he came back, and Denver held MoJo's attention rapt with a scrap of lunchmeat he dangled just out of her reach above her head.

"I'm trying to teach her to jump," he explained when El sat down next to him.

El watched his dog stare in confusion at the meat. "She's not going to jump. She's going to sit there waiting for you to give her the turkey."

"I disagree." Denver made clicking sounds and bounced the turkey up and down a few times, MoJo tracking the movement as if it were the most important thing in her life. "She'll figure it out eventually."

Somehow the whole world seemed wrapped up in MoJo figuring out she should leap up off her hind legs and snatch that lunchmeat. El didn't coo to her like Denver did, but he sat on the edge of his seat, gripping the plastic, teeth set. *Go get it. You know you want it. It's right there. Jump up and take it.*

"Come on, girl." Denver lowered the meat long enough for it to brush her nose, pulling it away as she tried to snap. "Come on. I won't even hold it that high. Stand on your hind legs, honey. You can do it."

Do it, damn it. You know you want it. Fucking take it!

MoJo continued to sit there, waiting patiently for Denver to move the turkey close enough for her to take it without leaping.

After ten excruciating minutes, El leapt to his feet like someone had put him on a spring. "I'm going to smoke."

"I'll have them get the iron lung ready for you when you get back," Denver replied. "Come on, girl."

Biting back an expletive, El headed for the door.

He didn't need anybody, he told himself as his shaking hands fumbled with the lighter, as he coughed up some disturbing phlegm and his mouth ached in dryness. It didn't matter what the fuck Paul did with his goddamned ring or if they were over before they'd even started. It didn't matter, because he'd always known it would end like this, and it was just as well it happened now rather than later.

"I don't need anybody, dammit," he murmured out loud, then swore and tossed his lighter and then his last three cigarettes against the wall before shutting his eyes and resting his head against the bricks.

CHAPTER 26

It should have been good, having my mom around to distract me while I tried to sort out why El had gotten so upset, why I still had no intention of taking that ring out of my bedside drawer, why part of me was devastated by his silence and part of me was relieved.

Having her around should have helped, but it didn't.

She had my entire house cleaned by the time I came home from work the first day she was there by herself, and a fresh loaf of bread and a rack of cooling cookies waited for me on the counter. I took her out to dinner that night and gave her a walking tour of the Light District, pointing out shops she might like to visit.

"Since you've already run out of things to clean at my place," I teased her.

She tweaked my nose, but she smiled too. "You've really cleaned up the clutter, I see. That's good. They say if your house is cluttered, so is your life."

I thought of the ring burning a hole in the back of my drawer and said nothing.

When I came home the second night, she had several bags on my kitchen counter from her shopping adventures, and she took me on a tour of where she'd bought them. "I got this bag at the cutest boutique on the corner by that coffee shop, and I got your father a new golf shirt and a pair of loafers for church. But wait until you hear this. I got this"—she pulled something out of a bag and presented me with my very own panini press—"for free! It was at this pawnshop, where the owner had the most darling little dog. I tried to pay him, and at first he was all set to take my credit card, but then all of a sudden he gave me this funny look and a wink and told me redheads got one item free today. I thought he had to be joking, but he wouldn't take so much as a penny no matter how I tried to pay. Oh—Paul, what's wrong?"

"Nothing," I lied. "Just tired from the day."

Mom patted me on the shoulder and kissed me on the cheek. "You poor thing. You go soak in a hot tub and let me fix you some dinner."

I took a shower, not a bath, but I stayed in there a long time, thinking of the time we'd had sex there. I'd thought of him all day, in fact, and all night, and all the time ever since he'd walked out the door. He hadn't so much as sent me a text, and I hadn't texted him either.

All because of that ring, that stupid, stupid ring.

While I was getting dressed, my phone rang. I leapt for it, thinking it would be El, and I tried to scramble an apology together, anything to get him back again, even though I still wasn't quite sure I'd actually lost him. Or had him in the first place.

My breath caught as I realized it wasn't El—it was Stacey.

"Hey there," she said when I greeted her. She sounded like she'd been crying. A lot. "I was wondering—could I come over? Just to talk?"

No. No, because I don't want El to find out you were here. "Um, my mom's here."

"Oh." That should have sent her off, no problem, so the fact that I could all but hear her trying to decide if she should still come over meant something big had happened. "Oh. Maybe you could meet me somewhere for a little while? There's something I need to say to you, and I can't do it over the phone."

No. No way, not in a million years. My grip on the phone became sweaty. "Mom's got dinner on."

Why couldn't I say it? Why couldn't I tell her no? Why was I even considering telling my mom something had come up and I'd be right back?

Why was that ring in my drawer? What the fuck was wrong with me?

"I want to come back to you," Stacey blurted out, her voice breaking on a sob. "Larry's cheating on me. I never should have been with him at all. I never should have left you. Please, Paul, can I please come home? I want to come home."

No. No, no, no, no, no! "Um . . ."

"Please," she whispered. "We can get married at the courthouse right away. I'll do whatever you want, only please take me back."

No! But another voice whispered, as desperate as Stacey, *Yes, oh yes, thank God, just tell her yes so everything can go back to normal.*

"Paul?" my mother called from the kitchen. "Paul, honey, dinner's ready."

"I have to go," I blurted into the phone, and hung up before I could change my mind.

Then I turned the phone off and buried it in my bedside drawer next to the ring.

"Paul, sweetheart. You look worse than when I sent you in to have your soak," Mom chided when I came to the dining room table. The lights flickered and the smoke alarm began to bleat. I got up wordlessly, climbed on a chair, took the battery out, and went back to my seat.

I stared at my plate for several seconds, hearing my mother's voice of concern as if from very far away. Eventually I lifted my head, looked at her, and said, "Mom, would you love me no matter what? No matter who I said I was or"—*what my orientation*—"whatever I thought would make me happy?"

It didn't surprise me when she teared up and sat down beside me, taking my hand and pressing it tight against her chest, over her warm and rapidly beating heart. "Yes. Absolutely." She said the words like a vow.

"No matter *what*?" I said, wishing I could let the cat out of the bag without letting her know there was a cat at all.

She caught my other hand too and drew it to her mouth. "Paul, sweetheart—yes. Yes, I will love you even though you're gay."

I blinked for several seconds, sure I couldn't have heard her right. Except I was also, contrarily, sure I had. "Mom?" I said, my voice cracking.

She made this funny cooing sound and stroked my cheek. "It's okay, baby. I know. I've always known."

"Mom, I haven't even said anything yet."

She hesitated. "Well—you *are* gay, yes?"

"I don't know!" I leaned back and shoved my hand into my damp hair. "How—?"

She laughed. "How did I know? Paul, I've known since you were eight and I caught you masturbating in front of the TV to Bo and Luke Duke."

If the battery had still been in the smoke alarm, I'm sure my face would have set it off again. I'd completely forgotten about that day, but I remembered now. "*Mom.*"

She stopped laughing, but her expression was calm and soothing as she petted my hand, my arm, my knee, whatever she could reach. "Sweetheart, it's okay. Of course I love you, and so does your father."

"*Dad* knows?" My voice was so high soon only dogs would be able to hear it. How in the hell was this happening to me? "How? *I* didn't even know until a few days ago. And I still don't even know. I think I might be bi."

"Whichever is fine, honey. So long as you're happy, that's what matters. Of course we didn't *know*, but yes, we suspected. All the literature told us to let you come to us with it, so we were waiting."

They'd been reading literature? "But I was engaged! To a woman!"

"You did say you might be bi, yes?" When I sputtered, she started patting me again. "It's all right, sweetheart. Does it matter what you are? Do you really need a label? Can't you just be Paul, who loves people however they come to him?" She winked at me. "Though I'd love to hear that bitch Stacey was just a phase."

I kept shaking my head, not knowing what to say. She moved her patting to my back.

"There, there, honey. Go ahead and breathe. I'm still here, and I still love you."

I pushed her hands away. "That was Stacey on the phone. She wants to come back to me. She begged me."

For the first time in the conversation, my mom frowned. "Have you tried porn, honey? I hear the Internet is full of it and that the gay stuff is really top notch."

"*Mom.*"

She flattened her lips. "Well, fine, but please don't take her back. That woman never loved you, not like you deserve. She used you and treated you like you were something she picked up at that pawnshop."

The knife that had been hovering over my chest ever since she'd unveiled that damn panini press drove right into my heart. "That—that's El, Mom. The guy who gave you the panini press. My . . . boyfriend."

Her face lit up like I'd told her I'd won ten million dollars. "Oh, sweetheart, that's wonderful! You need to get him to quit smoking, of course, but he was so charming, so kind. And so handsome. Why in the world are you thinking about taking Stacey back when you have him?"

I have no idea.

Except I did, and finally, finally the chipmunk let go of the question I'd been wanting to ask her ever since I came out of the bedroom. "But Mom, what if I don't *want* to be gay, or bi, or anything but normal?"

My mother's face turned to steel. "Paul Allan Hannon, you *are* normal. Who you are is not a choice. If you're gay or bi, you're gay or bi, and that's that. You can't choose to be straight if it isn't who you are." She searched my face a few moments, and then hers fell. "I should have told you that when you were younger, shouldn't I?"

I swallowed against a throat that was suddenly dry and scratchy. "Maybe."

She kissed me on the cheek, tears running down her face, and when she pulled back, I had tears too.

"Eat your dinner," she said, "and then we're going to go buy a few more things for this fantastic yard of yours. Then we're going to stay up late talking about boys, and girls too so long as they aren't Stacey, and tomorrow morning you're going to take me back to that shop and introduce me to your young man." She tweaked my nose again, smiling through her tears. "Come on. My scalloped potatoes aren't any good cold."

Letting go of a weight I thought I'd been carrying since that afternoon with the Hazzard boys, I picked up my fork and ate my mother's potatoes, dreaming tentative daydreams about making everything up to El in the morning.

CHAPTER 27

O n the night before the Fourth of July, Abuela called El over for an emergency meeting: Patti had found out they'd cleaned the attic.

Though he went straight over, by the time he and MoJo arrived, the hysterics were in full swing and the entire Rozal family was on the front lawn carrying on like a bad episode of *Cops*. In the center of it all was Patti, eyes swollen and nose running as she keened for her father's lost junk like someone mourning the dead.

She looked, he realized, like he felt when he thought about losing Paul.

For the first time in his life, as their gazes met and El saw the sorrow in his mother's face, as he felt it reflect the agony in his own heart, he understood the truth of his mother's pain: that mourning the dead and the lost was exactly what she was doing.

"Emanuel." She wiped her nose with her sleeve and pointed to his uncle. "Emanuel, they took his things. *They took his things.*"

Except this time he heard what she didn't say as well as the things she did. *They took him, Emanuel. They took my papi away.*

El swallowed hard and came closer to his mother, letting MoJo down to run after the kids. "I know, Mami. I'm sorry."

"They took his things," she sobbed again.

They took him. They took my papi.

Rosa glared at El, waiting for him to be rational. Lorenzo and Miguel only looked tired.

El closed the distance between his mother and himself and enfolded her into his arms. "They took his things," he whispered, "but they didn't take him."

Patricia Rozal shuddered, gripped El's shoulders, then sank heavily against him with a new round of sobs.

El held her, swaying from side to side as he let his mother cry. "It's just things. You don't need them to remember, Mami. He's bigger than that. And so are you."

"But I miss him," she sobbed.

"I know." El shut his eyes and thought of Paul hovering over him in bed and smiling. Paul blinking cluelessly as El flirted with him. Paul, eyes falling closed as he gave himself over to the pleasure El made for him.

Paul. Paul, who wasn't a thing at all, who El did need, who he missed very much. Paul, who was worth the risk of being disappointed, of being abandoned. Because even if it ended someday, if Paul left or they grew apart or something else, having him for a while would be better than not having him at all.

He crooned to his mother, smoothing her hair, promising himself as soon as this was settled that he'd drive across town to get Paul back.

Noah was there too, he realized as they finally convinced Patti she should sit down in her rocker (after Lorenzo cleaned out the crap from it and moved it into a space where it had room to rock) and drink some tea. When he asked Rosa about it, she shrugged.

"He was helping me set up and insisted he come over with me when I got the call from Abuela."

El glanced over at Noah, who watched, hovering and ready to jump in and comfort Rosa in case she needed it, or to get her a glass of water or the moon or whatever it was she decided she wanted. And El decided it had all gone far enough.

He turned his sister to face Noah, holding her firmly by the shoulders. "What is it you see, Rosa?"

"What the fuck, El?" She glared at him, but when he wouldn't budge, she sighed the sigh of the perpetually weary little sister. "I see Noah. So what?"

"Yes, Noah," El said. "Noah who babysits your kids whenever you ask him. Noah who buys you grills and patio sets and sets them up in your yard for you. Noah who came over tonight with you. Noah, who I would jump in a hot minute except he's straight and only, you might notice, has eyes for you."

Rosa went still. "No."

"Yes. I know you didn't meet him in a bar and that his IQ is fifty times higher than the slugs you usually hook up with, but you might want to give this one a try." She swatted at him, but only halfheartedly, too stunned and fixated on Noah, who was fixated right back and looking really, really hopeful. El kissed her on the cheek and patted her backside. "Go get him, tiger."

El wove his way through the backyard and the house. He was done pouting and being determined that Paul was going to go back to women or simply get tired of him. He'd find a way to make it work. He'd wait until Paul was ready to let go of the ring and anything else.

He'd adopt fifty dogs and maybe even a cat, if that's what it took.

His mother protested when he kissed her goodbye. "You just got here," she complained. "And Miguel already had to leave because he had to go to a fire."

"I know, Mami, but I'll be back tomorrow." He squeezed her hand and smiled, though it was a little shaky. "Maybe with a handsome young man on my arm."

His mother smiled broadly and squeezed his hand back. "You do that, Emanuel. You do that."

He kissed her soundly on the lips. "*Te amo, Mami.*"

"*Te amo, Emanuel,*" she whispered back, hugging him tight.

MoJo leaned enthusiastically out the driver's side window all the way over to Paul's side of town, and if El could've done it while driving, he would have, too. He settled for scratching her behind her ears instead. "Let's go see if we can find you another daddy, huh, sweetheart?" MoJo barked enthusiastically and wagged her tail.

El's heart beat hard as he rounded the corner to Paul's street.

But not half as hard as when he heard the sirens.

CHAPTER 28

"**I**s there supposed to be smoke like that?" Mom asked, pointing.

I craned my neck around the sun visor she'd lowered and squinted at the horizon just below the mountains, where indeed there was a nasty, black plume of smoke. "I don't think so. If someone's burning trash with this drought, they're going to get one hell of a fine."

"That's an awful lot of smoke to be a trash fire," Mom observed.

"Maybe the trash fire has already gotten out of hand," I said, hoping it wasn't on my block and that if it was, the fire trucks weren't blocking my house.

But when we turned onto my street, we found out the fire wasn't just on my block. It was my house.

My *house*. My house was *on fire*.

I didn't remember parking the car, only that one minute I was looking at fire roaring out of my house's windows, and the next I was on the street, a female firefighter holding me back as I stared, dumbfounded, at my life going up in flames.

Suddenly someone was hugging me hard and sobbing. It was Stacey.

"Oh, Paul." She buried her face in my shoulder. "Paul, our house!"

"Stacey, why are you here?" I wasn't even sure she actually was. Everything seemed muted and far away.

"I came over to talk to you, and the house was on fire! Oh, Paul, how could you let this happen?"

She was clinging hard to me, and I didn't like it. I pushed her off, and before she could reattach, my mother swooped in and drew her away. *Thanks, Mom.*

I went back to staring at my house, watching it burn.

It felt . . . oddly good.

Really good, actually, and the longer I watched, the better I felt. *Things. Just things*, El's voice whispered inside my head. All my things were burning up, and Stacey's too, everything we had built together, everything that was nothing more than a lie I never needed to have told. That and a couple of pairs of scrubs. And my phone. And my iPod.

Things.

I laughed, quietly, raising my hand to my mouth to hide my smile.

"*Paul.*"

It was El's voice again, but this time it wasn't in my head. It was behind me, and when I turned, there he was, face pale and eyes wide as he ran toward me, his shoes slapping against the water in the street.

"El," I said, smiling. "You're here."

You're here, and you're the only thing I really need.

He crushed me to him, holding me like he would never let me go. "You scared me half to death. I thought you were in there. I even called you, but you didn't pick up your phone."

"I left it in the house." I shut my eyes and pulled him closer. "El, I'm so sorry."

"You should be." He was shaking. "I thought I'd lost you."

"*Paul?*"

We both turned to Stacey, who stood next to my mother with eyes as big as her *Detroit Daisy*, watching the two of us embrace.

"That's Stacey," I told him.

He snorted. "You can so do better."

I shut my eyes and leaned into him. "I already have."

Mom and I went back to El's place that night. My landlord, who'd heard from the fire department that it had all started because of faulty wiring, looked very pale and kept trying to put us into a nice hotel. But El wouldn't let go of my arm, and my mother couldn't stop cooing over MoJo, who'd been very put out to be left in El's car while he'd run through the chaos to find me. Mom wouldn't take the bedroom, either, insisting she wanted to sleep on the couch so she could stay up and watch TV. When I pointed out El didn't have one, she swatted me on the butt and told me to go make things up with my young man.

I did as I was told.

It didn't take much effort, since as soon as the door closed behind us, El had me in his arms, kissing me so hard I couldn't breathe.

"I thought I'd lost you," he said for what had to be the fifteenth time.

"You didn't," I assured him, and held him close.

"About tomorrow." He stroked my hair as he spoke. "My family has this big picnic, and I'd love it if you came with me. You and your mom both."

"Okay," I said, smiling, and kissed him.

He blinked at me a minute, almost as if I'd surprised him. Then he let out a breath that almost sounded like relief. "And stay here for now, okay? We'll get a better bed for your mom, but—just stay, Paul, please."

I wasn't sure when I'd been this happy, and this was speaking as someone whose house had just burned down. "Yes," I said. Then I pushed him onto the bed and reminded him as best I could that I was right there and not planning to go anywhere.

That night I dreamed about Bo and Luke Duke doing a striptease for me, but when Luke took me into his arms, he turned into a beautiful woman, then into El, and we made love all night long. At some point the dream turned into reality, El crushing my mouth under his as he drove into me again and again and again. After that my sleep was deep and dreamless, probably the most peaceful sleep I ever had.

Even so, I woke early, just after dawn. El was dead to the world, and so was Mom. I should have gone back to bed, but I couldn't sleep, so I got up and padded around the kitchen, not sure what to do with myself. It was almost like something was nagging at the back of my mind, but I couldn't grasp what it was. When MoJo danced around my legs, I took her outside, and once I was there, I realized what was bothering me and what I had to do to fix it. When she was done with her business, I took her back upstairs, left a note on the kitchen counter, and went for a walk.

Bill was outside when I got to the ruins of my house, assessing the damage to his own property.

"Is everything okay?" I asked him, frowning at his ruined flowerbed. "Outside of this, I mean."

"It's all good," he assured me. "They soaked the garage pretty well, and everything smells a little like smoke, but it's all going to be okay." He grimaced. "Sorry you can't say the same."

I waved the worry away. "I guess we're both out of the contest now, huh?"

Bill looked confused. "Contest?"

"The Curb Appeal contest from the neighborhood association. For $500? You know, what Lorraine has been helping you with?"

When I said Lorraine's name, Bill's eyes darkened and he glanced back at his house. "What about Lorraine?"

Lorraine, I realized, was watching us from Bill's front porch, in what looked to be a borrowed robe.

Pieces of the puzzle fell finally into place, and I had to swallow a laugh. Bill didn't know about the contest. He hadn't been competing with me. I remembered the way he'd gloated at me that one day, how Lorraine had been hanging out with him all that week, defecting from my yard.

Well, he'd been competing with me, but not for $500.

"Nothing," I said at last, and smiled. "Just that I hope the two of you are very happy together."

The clouds left Bill's face, and he smiled too. "You take care, Paul. I'll let you know if I hear of another rental in the neighborhood."

"Thanks," I said, eyeing the wreckage of my house, identifying what I hoped was the remains of my bedside table. "But I'm kind of hoping to be living somewhere else." I nodded at him. "If you'll excuse me, there's one thing I'd like to see if I can find."

CHAPTER 29

E l woke to the sound of someone knocking on his bedroom door. Blinking in confusion, he sat up and looked around for Paul. He wasn't there. "Yeah?"

The door opened, and Paul came in, looking like a hot mess, covered in ash and grime and stinking of smoke. He had a funny look on his face. "I can't go with you to the picnic."

"Oh." El tried not to give away how disappointed he was. "Well, that's okay," he lied.

Paul shook his head. "I can't go with you, not until I take care of something. Because I have something to pawn."

"What?" El said, coming to full attention.

Paul sat down beside him and held out his hand. El frowned down at the molten mess for several seconds, but just when he was about to ask what the fuck was going on, he saw the gold smear across what looked like the remains of a cellphone. What could only be a diamond glinted from the center of the keypad.

El bit his cheek to stop his smile. "Are you selling or pawning?"

"Well, I don't want it back," Paul replied, not even bothering to hide his grin.

El took the melted mess from his lover and pretended to consider it, in part to let himself savor the moment. "I don't know how much it's worth. You held onto it too long, and the value's gone way down."

Paul's hand slid up El's leg. "If I can't sell it, maybe I could work out a trade?"

"Maybe." El set the cellphone and ring merger onto the bedside table and drew Paul onto his lap. "I could take it, but in exchange, you have to go to the picnic."

"Well, yes, that was what I meant—"

"I'm not done," El said, holding him off. "You have to come with me, and I get to introduce you as my boyfriend."

Paul was smiling now. "Okay."

"And then later we're going to go to Lights Out, and I'm going to wear you as arm candy all night and introduce you to my friends. Then I'm going to make out with you on the dance floor again, and on the patio, and probably we'll steal Jase's key so I can do you in his office. Then tomorrow I'm going to close the shop and spend the day getting to know your mother, because I really, really like her."

Paul was beaming. "Fine with me."

El's throat threatened to close, but he swallowed hard, and took Paul's face in his hands. "You're going to stay with me at least for now, and if you want I'll help hook you up with a reasonably sized apartment, but it's going to be close to the shop, and you aren't moving out until your mother has gone and I have fucked you and you've fucked me in every square inch of this place, and maybe down in the shop too."

"It's a deal."

The last bit stuck in El's throat, but he pushed it through. "I'm sorry I was such a dick about the ring, about making you rush. I kept worrying you'd come to your senses and ditch me."

Paul caught El's hand and kissed the back of it, holding El's gaze as he spoke. "All I want is to be with you, Emanuel. You aren't my first choice or my second choice. You're my only choice."

If Denver could have seen El right then, he'd have laughed his meaty head off at what a sappy moment he'd found himself in. It wasn't just happily ever after—it was the schmaltzy Disney ending, the old-school kind with the warbly-voiced opera singers and tinny orchestra swell.

El loved every moment of it.

Paul's expression became mock-serious. "So, about this trade. I really need to unload this. Tell me what you need. I'll agree to whatever terms you want, El. Just so long as I get to be with you."

"That's enough for me," El said, drew their mouths together, and sealed the bargain with a kiss.

Want more Tucker Springs?

Visit again with the titles listed below,
and read on for a sneak peek of Never a Hero.

Where Nerves End
by L.A. Witt

Dirty Laundry
by Heidi Cullinan

Covet thy Neighbor
by L.A. Witt

Never a Hero
by Marie Sexton

CHAPTER 1

I t took three years for me to convince myself I was in love with my downstairs neighbor. It only took one day for her to move out of my life.

It wasn't her fault. Not really. It wasn't as if I'd ever told her how I felt. In truth, I'd barely spoken to her at all, outside of the general pleasantries between neighbors when we passed on the walk or ran into each other in our shared backyard. But I'd watched her. Not in a stalker kind of way. But some days, when she was out in the garden, I'd sit on my porch and read so I could catch glimpses of her through the flowers as she knelt in the dirt, her fingers sunk into the cold Colorado soil.

But what had really made me love her was listening to her.

Her name was Regina, and she was a pianist. Not a concert pianist, or even an aspiring one. She had a day job somewhere in town, doing what, I didn't know, but for three years, I'd seen her leave at 7:45 and come home at 5:20. For an hour or so, she'd be out of my sight, in her own apartment below mine. But sometime around 6:30 or 7:00, she'd always start to play, and I'd lie on the couch in my living room, directly above her piano, and think about how I could learn to love a woman like her.

But now here she was, moving out.

I watched out my window as she loaded boxes into a truck. She had help. Two men and one woman. I barely noticed the woman, but I studied the men. One was smaller, studious looking, glasses perched on his nose. A bit twitchy about touching the boxes or going in the house. I dubbed him The Academic. The other was bigger. Huge, in fact. Clearly one of those men who spent hours in the gym. He lugged boxes out to the truck two and three at a time.

The Hero.

Not that he was Regina's hero, though. The men were obviously a couple, although I tried not to notice how happy they looked together. The lingering glances and the secret smiles. For three years, I'd lived only a few blocks from the Light District in Tucker Springs, and for three years, I'd told myself it wasn't the place for me. That all I needed was to meet the right woman, and maybe all those other thoughts that snuck into my head late at night would disappear. That she could help me erase the embarrassed regret of my high school years, and the loneliness that had haunted me since college. If Regina and I were a couple, I'd told myself, her playing would get me through the tough times. Whenever I'd start to wonder how it felt to be on my knees in front of another man, whenever I'd start to think about what I really wanted, I could turn to her and say, "Play something for me." And she'd smile at me, pleased that I wanted to hear her latest piece, and as her fingers would dance over the keys, teasing Bach or Beethoven or Mozart from that big square box, I'd fall in love with her again and forget about the fact that it was men who turned my head, time and again.

Except now she was moving.

I pulled the shade down and turned away. I didn't want to watch her leave.

I also didn't want to watch two men who could openly admit they were in love.

"Owen, you're an idiot," I told myself. After all, a braver man would have offered to help. A more confident man would have taken this last opportunity to talk to her. Maybe get her phone number. A forwarding address, in case there was mail or a package. In case she wanted to have dinner some night. A whole man would have offered to help her move. An undamaged man wouldn't have been afraid to walk out and say, "Hey, let me lend you a hand."

I laughed suddenly at my own thoughts. How ironic that I'd think of one of my least-favorite phrases in the English language. I didn't exactly have an extra hand to spare.

I looked down at my left arm, where it ended in a smooth tapered stump just below my elbow.

"Let me lend you a hand," I said out loud. "But only if you give it back when you're done."

It wasn't as absurd as it sounded. I could have helped. It wasn't like I was incapable of carrying a damn box. Not two or three at a time, like The Hero, but that didn't make me worthless.

No, it wasn't my missing arm that stopped me from helping Regina move. It was the way they'd all react, sorting carefully through the boxes, deciding which ones I could carry. Nothing too heavy. Nothing breakable. Certainly not the glassware, or the boxes of books. Linens, though. Linens they might let me carry.

Or pillows. Even a one-armed man could carry pillows.

I'd never be anybody's hero.

"Stop feeling sorry for yourself," I muttered.

I was startled by a knock on the door. I was even more surprised to open it and find Regina on the other side. I stood as I always did, with the left half of my body hidden behind the door. Certainly she knew by now about my missing arm, but I'd learned people didn't like to see it.

"Hi, Erwin!" she said. It was an indicator of how little we'd actually talked. She didn't even know my name.

I was slow to answer, making sure my tongue was ready to move. I'd beaten my stutter years ago, but it still appeared sometimes. Usually at the least-opportune moments. "Ready to go?" I asked her, gesturing toward the truck.

"Yep, this is it!" She held a set of keys out for me. "I told the landlord I'd leave the spares with you."

I held out my right hand and let the keys fall into my palm. I thought about the one thing I hadn't seen The Hero carry out her door. "What about your piano?"

She shrugged and ran a hand through her short hair. There was more gray in it than I'd realized. When I'd imagined a life with her, I'd made her my age, but I was reminded now of the fact that she was actually more than ten years my senior, although she looked damn good for her age. "I'm leaving it. It wasn't mine to begin with. It belonged to whoever lived here before me, and anyway, it'd be a pain in the ass to move."

"Will you buy a new one?"

"I don't know. Maybe eventually. But mostly it takes up space and gathers dust, you know?"

She'd played almost every night. Certainly she loved it. I'd made myself believe she loved it. How else could I possibly love her?

"Anyway," she said, suddenly awkward. "Take care."

Take care.

Then she turned around and walked away. Down the sidewalk to the truck. Away from the imaginary life she'd unknowingly starred in.

Away from me.

Available now at Riptide Publishing.

Acknowledgments

Thanks to Hillari Hoerschelman and Jill Sorenson for Spanish help; and to Dan, Signy, and Rowan Speedwell for being the ultimate betas, as usual.

ALSO BY
HEIDI CULLINAN

Dirty Laundry: A Tucker Springs Novel
Hero
Special Delivery
Double Blind
The Wounds in the Walls
Miles and the Magic Flute
Sweet Son
Nowhere Ranch
Dance With Me
The Seventh Veil
Temple Boy
The Pirate's Game
A Private Gentleman
Family Man, with Marie Sexton

ALSO BY
MARIE SEXTON

Never a Hero: A Tucker Springs Novel
Promises
A to Z
The Letter Z
Strawberries for Dessert
Paris A to Z
Putting Out Fires
One More Soldier
Between Sinners and Saints
Song of Oestend
Saviours of Oestend
Blind Space
Cinder
Family Man, with Heidi Cullinan
Fear, Hope, and Bread Pudding (coming June 2013)

ABOUT
THE AUTHORS

Heidi Cullinan has always loved a good love story, provided it has a happy ending. She enjoys writing across many genres but loves above all to write happy, romantic endings for LGBT characters because there just aren't enough of those stories out there. When Heidi isn't writing, she enjoys cooking, reading, knitting, listening to music, and watching television with her husband and ten-year-old daughter. Heidi also volunteers frequently for her state's LGBT rights group, One Iowa, and is proud to be from the first midwestern state to legalize same-sex marriage.

Find out more about Heidi, including her social networks, at www.heidicullinan.com.

Marie Sexton lives in Colorado. She's a fan of just about anything that involves muscular young men piling on top of each other. In particular, she loves the Denver Broncos and enjoys going to the games with her husband. Her imaginary friends often tag along. Marie has one daughter, two cats, and one dog, all of whom seem bent on destroying what remains of her sanity. She loves them anyway.

You can find Marie on Twitter, and at mariesexton.net, or download the official Marie Sexton app (available free on iPhone and Android).

Facebook: www.facebook.com/MarieSexton.author
Twitter: twitter.com/MarieSexton
Get the app!
iOS: tiny.cc/mariesexton_apple
Android: tiny.cc/mariesexton_droid

Enjoyed this book?
Visit RiptidePublishing.com
to find more true love!

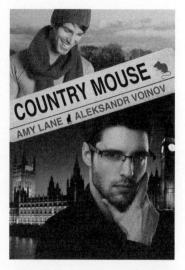

It isn't true love
until someone gets hurt.
ISBN: 978-1-937551-85-8

Country mouse meets city cat.
ISBN: 978-1-937551-34-6

Earn Bonus Bucks!

Earn 1 Bonus Buck for each dollar you spend. Find out how at RiptidePublishing.com/news/bonus-bucks.

Win Free Ebooks for a Year!

Pre-order coming soon titles directly through our site and you'll receive one entry into a drawing to win free books for a year! Get the details at RiptidePublishing.com/contests.